NATASHA

David Bezmozgis was born in Riga, Latvia, in 1973. In 1980 he emigrated with his parents to Toronto, where he lives today. This is his first book.

NATASHA

AND OTHER STORIES

·

DAVID BEZMOZGIS

JONATHAN CAPE · LONDON

Published by Jonathan Cape 2004

2 4 6 8 10 9 7 5 3 1

Grateful acknowledgement is made to the editors of the following magazines, in
whose pages these stories originally appeared in slightly different form: *Grain,
Harper's, paperplates, Prairie Fire, The New Yorker, The Walrus* and *Zoetrope*

First published in Great Britain in 2004 by
Jonathan Cape
Random House, 20 Vauxhall Bridge Road, London SW1V 2SA

Random House Australia (Pty) Limited
20 Alfred Street, Milsons Point, Sydney,
New South Wales 2061, Australia

Random House New Zealand Limited
18 Poland Road, Glenfield,
Auckland 10, New Zealand

Random House South Africa (Pty) Limited
Endulini, 5A Jubilee Road, Parktown 2193, South Africa

The Random House Group Limited Reg. No. 954009
www.randomhouse.co.uk

ISBN 0-224-07125-4

Papers used by Random House are natural,
recyclable products made from wood grown in sustainable forests;
the manufacturing processes conform to the environmental
regulations of the country of origin

Designed by Abby Kagan

Printed and bound in Great Britain by
Mackays of Chatham Plc, Chatham, Kent

*The author wishes to thank his agent, Ira Silverberg, for his faith and wise counsel, and his editor,
Lorin Stein, for the clarity and consistency of his editorial vision*

TO MY PARENTS

CONTENTS

TAPKA

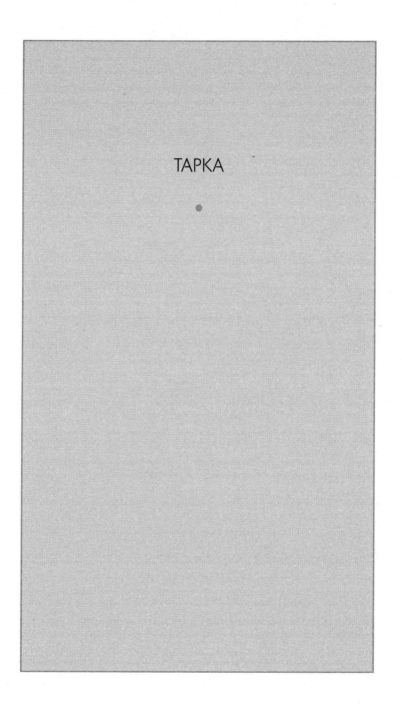

GOLDFINCH WAS FLAPPING CLOTHESLINES, a tenement delirious with striving. 6030 Bathurst: insomniac scheming Odessa. Cedarcroft: reeking borscht in the hallways. My parents, Baltic aristocrats, took an apartment at 715 Finch fronting a ravine and across from an elementary school—one respectable block away from the Russian swarm. We lived on the fifth floor, my cousin, aunt, and uncle directly below us on the fourth. Except for the Nahumovskys, a couple in their fifties, there were no other Russians in the building. For this privilege, my parents paid twenty extra dollars a month in rent.

In March of 1980, near the end of the school year but only three weeks after our arrival in Toronto, I was enrolled in Charles H. Best elementary. Each morning, with our house key hanging from a brown shoelace around my neck, I kissed my parents goodbye and, along with my cousin Jana, tramped across the ravine—I to the first grade, she to the second. At three o'clock, bearing the germs of a new vocabulary, we tramped back home. Together, we then waited until six for our parents to return from George Brown City College, where they were taking their obligatory classes in English.

In the evenings we assembled and compiled our linguistic bounty.

Hello, havaryew?

Red, yellow, green, blue.

May I please go to the washroom?

Seventeen, eighteen, nineteen, twenny.

Joining us most nights were the Nahumovskys. They attended the same English classes and traveled with my parents on the same bus. Rita Nahumovsky was a beautician, her face spackled with makeup, and Misha Nahumovsky was a tool and die maker. They came from Minsk and didn't know a soul in Canada. With abounding enthusiasm, they incorporated themselves into our family. My parents were glad to have them. Our life was tough, we had it hard—but the Nahumovskys had it harder. They were alone, they were older, they were stupefied by the demands of language. Being essentially helpless themselves, my parents found it gratifying to help the more helpless Nahumovskys.

After dinner, as we gathered on cheap stools around our table, my mother repeated the day's lessons for the benefit of the Nahumovskys and, to a slightly lesser degree, for the benefit of my father. My mother had always been a dedicated student and she extended this dedication to George Brown City College. My father and the Nahumovskys came to rely on her detailed notes and her understanding of the curriculum. For as long as they could, they listened attentively and groped toward comprehension. When this became too frustrating, my father put on the kettle, Rita painted my mother's nails, and Misha told Soviet jokes.

In a first-grade classroom a teacher calls on her students and inquires after their nationality. "Sasha," she says. Sasha says, "Russian." "Very good," says the teacher. "Arnan," she says. Arnan says, "Armenian." "Very good," says the teacher. "Lubka," she says. Lubka says, "Ukrainian." "Very good," says the teacher. And then she asks Dima. Dima says, "Jewish." "What a shame," says the teacher, "so young and already a Jew."

TAPKA

. . .

The Nahumovskys had no children, only a white Lhasa-apso named Tapka. The dog had lived with them for years before they emigrated and then traveled with them from Minsk to Vienna, from Vienna to Rome, and from Rome to Toronto. During our first month in the building, Tapka was in quarantine and I saw her only in photographs. Rita had dedicated an entire album to the dog, and to dampen the pangs of separation, she consulted the album daily. There were shots of Tapka in the Nahumovskys' old Minsk apartment, seated on the cushions of faux Louis XIV furniture; there was Tapka on the steps of a famous Viennese palace; Tapka at the Vatican; in front of the Coliseum; at the Sistine Chapel; and under the Leaning Tower of Pisa. My mother—despite having grown up with goats and chickens in her yard—didn't like animals and found it impossible to feign interest in Rita's dog. Shown a picture of Tapka, my mother wrinkled her nose and said "foo." My father also couldn't be bothered. With no English, no money, no job, and only a murky conception of what the future held, he wasn't equipped to admire Tapka on the Italian Riviera. Only I cared. Through the photographs I became attached to Tapka and projected upon her the ideal traits of the dog I did not have. Like Rita, I counted the days until Tapka's liberation.

The day Tapka was to be released from quarantine Rita prepared an elaborate dinner. My family was invited to celebrate the dog's arrival. While Rita cooked, Misha was banished from their apartment. For distraction, he seated himself at our table with a deck of cards. As my mother reviewed sentence construction, Misha played hand after hand of Durak with me.

—The woman loves this dog more than me. A taxi to the customs facility is going to cost us ten, maybe fifteen dollars. But what can I do? The dog is truly a sweet little dog.

When it came time to collect the dog, my mother went with Misha and Rita to act as their interpreter. With my nose to the window, I watched the taxi take them away. Every few minutes, I reapplied my nose to the window. Three hours later the taxi pulled into our parking lot and Rita emerged from the back seat cradling animated fur. She set the fur down on the pavement, where it assumed the shape of a dog. The length of its coat concealed its legs, and as it hovered around Rita's ankles, it appeared to have either a thousand tiny legs or none at all. My head ringing "Tapka, Tapka, Tapka," I raced into the hallway to meet the elevator.

That evening Misha toasted the dog:

—This last month, for the first time in years, I have enjoyed my wife's undivided attention. But I believe no man, not even one as perfect as me, can survive so much attention from his wife. So I say, with all my heart, thank God our Tapka is back home with us. Another day and I fear I may have requested a divorce.

Before he drank, Misha dipped his pinkie finger into his vodka glass and offered it to the dog. Obediently, Tapka gave Misha's finger a thorough licking. Duly impressed, my uncle declared her a good Russian dog. He also gave her a lick of his vodka. I gave her a piece of my chicken. Jana rolled her a pellet of bread. Misha taught us how to dangle food just out of Tapka's reach and thereby induce her to perform a charming little dance. Rita also produced "Clonchik," a red and yellow rag clown. She tossed Clonchik under the table, onto the couch, down the hallway, and into the kitchen; over and over

Rita called, "Tapka get Clonchik," and, without fail, Tapka got Clonchik. Everyone delighted in Tapka's antics except for my mother, who sat stiffly in her chair, her feet slightly off the ground, as though preparing herself for a mild electric shock.

After the dinner, when we returned home, my mother announced that she would no longer set foot in the Nahumovskys' apartment. She liked Rita, she liked Misha, but she couldn't sympathize with their attachment to the dog. She understood that the attachment was a consequence of their lack of sophistication and also their childlessness. They were simple people. Rita had never attended university. She could derive contentment from talking to a dog, brushing its coat, putting ribbons in its hair, and repeatedly throwing a rag clown across the apartment. And Misha, although very lively and a genius with his hands, was also not an intellectual. They were good people, but a dog ruled their lives.

Rita and Misha were sensitive to my mother's attitude toward Tapka. As a result, and to the detriment of her progress with English, Rita stopped visiting our apartment. Nightly, Misha would arrive alone while Rita attended to the dog. Tapka never set foot in our home. This meant that, in order to see her, I spent more and more time at the Nahumovskys'. Each evening, after I had finished my homework, I went to play with Tapka. My heart soared every time Rita opened the door and Tapka raced to greet me. The dog knew no hierarchy of affection. Her excitement was infectious. In Tapka's presence I resonated with doglike glee.

Because of my devotion to the dog and their lack of an alternative, Misha and Rita added their house key to the shoelace hanging around my neck. Every day, during our lunch break and again after school, Jana and I were charged with caring for Tapka. Our task was simple: put Tapka on her leash, walk her to the ravine, release her to chase Clonchik, and then bring her home.

Every day, sitting in my classroom, understanding little, effectively friendless, I counted down the minutes to lunchtime. When the bell rang I met Jana on the playground and we sprinted across the grass toward our building. In the hall, our approaching footsteps elicited panting and scratching. When I inserted the key into the lock I felt emanations of love through the door. And once the door was open, Tapka hurled herself at us, her entire body consumed with an ecstasy of wagging. Jana and I took turns embracing her, petting her, covertly vying for her favor. Free of Rita's scrutiny, we also satisfied certain anatomical curiosities. We examined Tapka's ears, her paws, her teeth, the roots of her fur, and her doggy genitals. We poked and prodded her, we threw her up in the air, rolled her over and over, and swung her by her front legs. I felt such overwhelming love for Tapka that sometimes when hugging her, I had to restrain myself from squeezing too hard and crushing her little bones.

It was April when we began to care for Tapka. Snow melted in the ravine; sometimes it rained. April became May. Grass absorbed the thaw, turned green; dandelions and wildflowers sprouted yellow and blue; birds and insects flew, crawled, and made their characteristic noises. Faithfully and reliably, Jana and I attended to Tapka. We walked her across the parking lot and down into the ravine. We threw Clonchik and said "Tapka get Clonchik." Tapka always got Clonchik. Everyone was proud of us. My mother and my aunt wiped tears from their eyes while talking about how responsible we were. Rita and Misha rewarded us with praise and chocolates. Jana was seven and I was six; much had been asked of us, but we had risen to the challenge.

Inspired by everyone's confidence, we grew confident. Whereas at first we made sure to walk thirty paces into the ravine before releasing Tapka, we gradually reduced that requirement to ten paces, then five paces, until finally we released her at the grassy border between the parking lot and ravine. We did this not out of laziness or recklessness but because we wanted proof of Tapka's love. That she came when we called was evidence of her love, that she didn't piss in the elevator was evidence of her love, that she offered up her belly for scratching was evidence of her love, all of this was evidence, but it wasn't proof. Proof could come only in one form. We had intuited an elemental truth: love needs no leash.

That first spring, even though most of what was said around me remained a mystery, a thin rivulet of meaning trickled into my cerebral catch basin and collected into a little pool of knowledge. By the end of May I could sing the ABC song. Television taught me to say "What's up, Doc?" and "superduper." The playground introduced me to "shithead," "mental case," and "gaylord," and I sought every opportunity to apply my new knowledge.

One afternoon, after spending nearly an hour in the ravine throwing Clonchik in a thousand different directions, Jana and I lolled in the sunlit pollen. I called her "shithead," "mental case," and "gaylord," and she responded by calling me "gaylord," "shithead," and "mental case."

—Shithead.

—Gaylord.

—Mental case.

—Tapka, get Clonchik.

—Shithead.

—Gaylord.

—Come, Tapka-lapka.

—Mental case.

We went on like this, over and over, until Jana threw the clown and said, "Shithead, get Clonchik." Initially, I couldn't tell if she had said this on purpose or if it had merely been a blip in her rhythm. But when I looked at Jana, her smile was triumphant.

—Mental case, get Clonchik.

For the first time, as I watched Tapka bounding happily after Clonchik, the profanity sounded profane.

—Don't say that to the dog.

—Why not?

—It's not right.

—But she doesn't understand.

—You shouldn't say it.

—Don't be a baby. Come, shithead, come, my dear one.

Her tail wagging with accomplishment, Tapka dropped Clonchik at my feet.

—You see, she likes it.

I held Clonchik as Tapka pawed frantically at my shins.

—Call her shithead. Throw the clown.

—I'm not calling her shithead.

—What are you afraid of, shithead?

I aimed the clown at Jana's head and missed.

—Shithead, get Clonchik.

As the clown left my hand, Tapka, a white shining blur, oblivious to insult, was already cutting through the grass. I wanted to believe that I had intended the "shithead" exclusively for Jana, but I knew it wasn't true.

—I told you, gaylord, she doesn't care.

I couldn't help thinking, "Poor Tapka," and looked around for some sign of recrimination. The day, however, persisted in unimpeachable brilliance: sparrows winged overhead; bumblebees levitated above flowers; beside a lilac shrub, Tapka clamped down on Clonchik. I was amazed at the absence of consequences.

Jana said, "I'm going home."

As she started for home I saw that she was still holding Tapka's leash. It swung insouciantly from her hand. I called after her just as, once again, Tapka deposited Clonchik at my feet.

—I need the leash.

—Why?

—Don't be stupid. I need the leash.

—No you don't. She comes when we call her. Even shithead. She won't run away.

Jana turned her back on me and proceeded toward our building. I called her again but she refused to turn around. Her receding back was a blatant provocation. Guided more by anger than by logic, I decided that if Tapka was closer to Jana, then the onus of responsibility would become hers. I picked up the doll and threw it as far as I could into the parking lot.

—Tapka, get Clonchik.

Clonchik tumbled through the air. I had put everything in my six-year-old arm behind the throw, which still meant that the doll wasn't going very far. Its trajectory promised a drop no more than twenty feet from the edge of the ravine. Running, her head arched to the sky, Tapka tracked the flying clown. As the doll reached its apex it crossed paths with a sparrow. The bird veered off toward Finch Avenue and the clown plummeted to the asphalt. When the doll hit the ground, Tapka raced past it after the bird.

A thousand times we had thrown Clonchik and a thousand times Tapka had retrieved him. But who knows what passes for a thought in the mind of a dog? One moment a Clonchik is a Clonchik and the next moment a sparrow is a Clonchik.

I shouted at Jana to catch Tapka and then watched as the dog, her attention fixed on the sparrow, skirted past Jana and into traffic. From the slope of the ravine I couldn't see what had happened. I saw only that Jana had broken into a sprint and I heard the caterwauling of tires followed by a shrill fractured yip.

By the time I reached the street a line of cars was already stretched a block beyond Goldfinch. At the front of the line were a brown station wagon and a pale blue sedan blistered with rust. As I neared, I noted the chrome letters on the back of the sedan: D-U-S-T-E-R. In front of the sedan Jana kneeled in a tight semicircle with a pimply young man and an older woman wearing very large sunglasses. Tapka lay panting on her side at the center of their circle. She stared at me, at Jana. Except for a hind leg twitching at the sky at an impossible angle, she looked much as she did when she rested on the rug at the Nahumovskys' apartment after a romp in the ravine.

Seeing her this way, barely mangled, I started to convince myself that things weren't as bad as I had feared and I edged forward to pet her. The woman in the sunglasses said something in a restrictive tone that I neither understood nor heeded. I placed my hand on Tapka's head and she responded by turning her face and allowing a trickle of blood to escape onto the asphalt. This was the first time I had ever seen dog blood and I was struck by the depth of its color. I hadn't expected it to be red, although I also hadn't expected it to be not-red. Set against the gray asphalt and her white coat, Tapka's blood was the red I envisioned when I closed my eyes and thought: red.

I sat with Tapka until several dozen car horns demanded that we clear the way. The woman with the large sunglasses ran to her station wagon, returned with a blanket, and scooped Tapka off the street. The pimply young man stammered a few sentences of which I understood nothing except the word "sorry." Then we were in the back seat of the station wagon with Tapka in Jana's lap. The woman kept talking until she realized that we couldn't understand her at all. As we started to drive, Jana remembered something. I motioned for the woman to stop the car and scrambled out. Above the atonal chorus of car horns I heard:

—Mark, get Clonchik.

I ran and got Clonchik.

For two hours Jana and I sat in the reception area of a small veterinary clinic in an unfamiliar part of town. In another room, with a menagerie of various afflicted creatures, Tapka lay in traction, connected to a blinking machine by a series of tubes. Jana and I had been allowed to see her once but were rushed out when we both burst into tears. Tapka's doctor, a woman in a white coat and furry slippers resembling bear paws, tried to calm us down. Again, we could neither explain ourselves nor understand what she was saying. We managed only to establish that Tapka was not our dog. The doctor gave us coloring books, stickers, and access to the phone. Every fifteen minutes we called home. Between phone calls we absently flipped pages and sniffled for Tapka and for ourselves. We had no idea what would happen to Tapka, all we knew was that she wasn't dead. As for ourselves, we already felt punished and knew only that more punishment was to come.

—Why did you throw Clonchik?

—Why didn't you give me the leash?

—You could have held on to her collar.

—You shouldn't have called her shithead.

At six-thirty my mother picked up the phone. I could hear the agitation in her voice. The ten minutes she had spent at home not knowing where I was had taken their toll. For ten minutes she had been the mother of a dead child. I explained to her about the dog and felt a twinge of resentment when she said "So it's just the dog?" Behind her I heard other voices. It sounded as though everyone was speaking at once, pursuing personal agendas, translating the phone conversation from Russian to Russian until one anguished voice separated itself: "My God, what happened?" Rita.

After getting the address from the veterinarian my mother hung up and ordered another expensive taxi. Within a half hour my parents, my aunt, and Misha and Rita pulled up at the clinic. Jana and I waited for them on the sidewalk. As soon as the taxi doors opened we began to sob. Partly out of relief but mainly in the hope of eliciting sympathy. As I ran to my mother I caught sight of Rita's face. Her face made me regret that I also hadn't been hit by a car.

As we clung to our mothers, Rita descended upon us.

—Children, what oh what have you done?

She pinched compulsively at the loose skin of her neck, raising a cluster of pink marks.

While Misha methodically counted individual bills for the taxi driver, we swore on our lives that Tapka had simply gotten away from us. That we had minded her as always, but, inexplicably, she had seen a bird and bolted from the ravine and into the road. We had done everything in our power to catch her, but she had surprised us, eluded us, been too fast.

Rita considered our story.

—You are liars. Liars!

She uttered the words with such hatred that we again burst into sobs.

My father spoke in our defense.

—Rita Borisovna, how can you say this? They are children.

—They are liars. I know my Tapka. Tapka never chased birds. Tapka never ran from the ravine.

—Maybe today she did?

—Liars.

Having delivered her verdict, she had nothing more to say. She waited anxiously for Misha to finish paying the driver.

—Misha, enough already. Count it a hundred times, it will still be the same.

Inside the clinic there was no longer anyone at the reception desk. During our time there, Jana and I had watched a procession of dyspeptic cats and lethargic parakeets disappear into the back rooms for examination and diagnosis. One after another they had come and gone until, by the time of our parents' arrival, the waiting area was entirely empty and the clinic officially closed. The only people remaining were a night nurse and the doctor in the bear paw slippers who had stayed expressly for our sake.

Looking desperately around the room, Rita screamed: "Doctor! Doctor!" But when the doctor appeared she was incapable of making herself understood. Haltingly, with my mother's help, it was communicated to the doctor that Rita wanted to see her dog.

Pointing vigorously at herself, Rita asserted: "Tapka. Mine dog."

The doctor led Rita and Misha into the veterinary version of an intensive care ward. Tapka lay on her little bed, Clonchik resting directly beside her. At the sight of Rita and Misha, Tapka weakly wagged her tail. Little more than an hour had elapsed since I had seen her last, but somehow over the course of that time, Tapka had shrunk considerably. She had always been a small dog, but now she looked desiccated. Rita started to cry, grotesquely smearing her mascara. With trembling hands, and with sublime tenderness, she stroked Tapka's head.

—My God, my God, what has happened to you, my Tapkachka?

Through my mother, and with the aid of pen and paper, the doctor provided the answer. Tapka required two operations. One for her leg. Another to stop internal bleeding. An organ had been damaged. For now, a machine was helping her, but without the machine she would die. On the paper the doctor drew a picture of a scalpel, of a dog, of a leg, of an organ. She made an arrow pointing at the organ and drew a teardrop and colored it in to represent "blood." She also wrote down a number preceded by a dollar sign. The number was 1,500.

At the sight of the number Rita let out a low animal moan and steadied herself against Tapka's little bed. My parents exchanged a glance. I looked at the floor. Misha said, "My dear God." The Nahumovskys and my parents each took in less than five hundred dollars a month. We had arrived in Canada with almost nothing, a few hundred dollars, but that had all but disappeared on furniture. There were no savings. Fifteen hundred dollars. The doctor could just as well have written a million.

In the middle of the intensive care ward, Rita slid down to the floor. Her head thrown back, she appealed to the fluorescent lights: "Nu, Tapkachka, what is going to become of us?"

I looked up from my feet and saw horror and bewilderment on the doctor's face. She tried to put a hand on Rita's shoulder but Rita violently shrugged it off.

My father attempted to intercede.

—Nu, Rita Borisovna, I understand that it is painful, but it is not the end of the world.

—And what do you know about it?

—I know that it must be hard, but soon you will see . . . Even tomorrow we could go and help you find a new one.

My father looked to my mother for approval, to ensure that he had not promised too much.

—A new one? What do you mean a new one? I don't want a new one. Why don't you get yourself a new son? A new little liar? How about that? New. Everything we have now is new.

On the linoleum floor, Rita keened, rocking back and forth. She hiccuped, as though hyperventilating. Pausing for a moment, she looked up at my mother and told her to translate to the doctor. To tell her that she would not let Tapka die.

—I will sit here on this floor forever. And if the police come to drag me out I will bite them.

—Ritachka, this is crazy.

—Why is it crazy? My Tapka's life is worth more than fifteen hundred dollars. Because we don't have the money she should die here? It's not her fault.

Seeking rationality, my mother turned to Misha. Misha, who had said nothing all this time except "My dear God."

—Misha, do you want me to tell the doctor what Rita said?

Misha shrugged philosophically.

—Tell her or don't tell her, you see my wife has made up her mind. The doctor will figure it out soon enough.

—And you think this is reasonable?

—Sure. Why not? I'll sit on the floor too. The police can take us both to jail. Besides Tapka, what else do we have?

Misha sat on the floor beside his wife.

I watched as my mother struggled to explain to the doctor what was happening. With a mixture of words and gesticulations she got the point across. The doctor, after considering her options, sat down on the floor beside Rita and Misha. Once again she tried to put her hand on Rita's shoulder. This time, Rita, who was still rocking back and forth, allowed it. Misha rocked in time to his wife's rhythm. So did the doctor. The three of them sat in a line, swaying together like campers at a campfire. Nobody said anything. We looked at each other. I watched Rita, Misha, and the doctor swaying and swaying. I became mesmerized by the swaying. I wanted to know what would happen to Tapka; the swaying answered me.

The swaying said: Listen, shithead, Tapka will live. The doctor will perform the operation. Either money will be found or money will not be necessary.

I said to the swaying: This is very good. I love Tapka. I meant her no harm. I want to be forgiven.

The swaying replied: There is reality and then there is truth. The reality is that Tapka will live. But let's be honest, the truth is you killed Tapka. Look at Rita; look at Misha. You see, who are you kidding? You killed Tapka and you will never be forgiven.

ROMAN BERMAN, MASSAGE THERAPIST

NIGHT AFTER NIGHT for more than a year, my father tortured himself with medical texts and dictionaries. After a long day at the chocolate bar factory he would come home and turn on the lamp in the bedroom. He would eat his soup with us in the kitchen, but he'd take the main course into the bedroom, resting his plate on a rickety Soviet stool. The work was difficult. He was approaching fifty, and the English language was more an enemy than an instrument. In Latvia, after resigning from the Ministry of Sport, my father had made a living as a masseur in the sanatoriums along the Baltic coast. He'd needed no accreditation, only some minimal training and the strength of his connections. But in the new country, to get his certificate, he was forced to memorize complex medical terminology and to write an eight-hour exam in a foreign language.

Getting his license would mean that he could start his own business. At the time, aside from the chocolate bar factory, he also worked at the Italian Community Center, where he massaged mobsters and manufacturers and trained seven amateur weightlifters. The money was lousy, but he was making contacts. He was certain he could take some of the Italians with him if he started his own practice. And if he got his office in just the right location, the old Polish Jews would surely follow. This was 1983, and as Russian Jews, recent immigrants, and political refugees, we were still a cause. We had good PR. We could trade on our history.

The morning my father was to write the exam, my mother made an omelette and quartered a tomato. He ate quickly, downing his tea. His bare feet set a steady rhythm going in and out, in and out of his slippers. I told him about tryouts for indoor soccer. I described the fuzzy yellow ball. Midway through the omelette, he got up and retched into the sink.

He left the apartment stolidly, as if he were going off to war. In a rare moment of overt affection, my mother gave him a kiss. My parents hugged in the hallway, because it is bad luck to kiss someone at the threshold.

At the window, I watched as he backed the massive green Pontiac out of the parking lot. It was the end of March and still cold. The heater in the car didn't work, and as my mother joined me at the window, we could see the long streams of my father's condensed breathing as he turned onto Finch Avenue.

"God willing, God willing," my mother said.

Three weeks later we received the letter from the Board of Directors of Masseurs. A certificate would follow shortly, the sort of thing my father would frame and hang in his office. We celebrated the news by going to the Pizza Patio restaurant in a strip mall not far from our apartment building. I spoke for the family and ordered a large pepperoni and mushroom pizza. We toasted to our future with fountain Cokes.

The next weekend my father signed a lease for a one-room office at the Sunnybrook Plaza, where we bought our groceries and I got my hair cut. For eighty dollars, Yuri from Smolensk built a sturdy massage table wrapped in burgundy Naugahyde and secured with shiny brass rivets. My father paid half that for a desk at a consignment shop in the East End, and ten bucks apiece for two used office chairs for the waiting area. On the recommendation of someone at the Italian Community Center, he also took out a one-year subscription to

Reader's Digest. And to create the impression of clinical privacy, we drove to Starkman's Medical Supply on Davenport where my father bought a green three-paneled room divider. The final touches were made by my mother, who purchased a sheet of adhesive letters from the hardware store and carefully spelled on the door: Roman Berman, Massage Therapist, BA, RMT.

After the initial excitement subsided, the reality of the situation asserted itself. Aside from the handful of Italians at the Community Center and some of my parents' Russian friends, nobody else knew that Roman's Therapeutic Massage existed. Boris Krasnansky from Tashkent, whose employer offered a modest benefits package, was my father's first patient. He went for as long as his benefits held out and insisted that my father kick back a third of the money since he was doing him a favor. Joe Galatti, a dry goods wholesaler, showed up each time with a bottle of homemade wine and told my father about his troubles with his son. Joe had a heavy Italian accent and my father's English was improving only slowly. The session would end only when the bottle was empty. Sal, a semi-retired contractor, came with his wife's cousin, who had arrived from Naples and fallen off a scaffold after his first week on the job. The cousin spoke no English and couldn't drive a car. Sal felt guilty and drove the cousin over on Saturday afternoons to give his wife a break. My father would massage the cousin, and Sal would sit outside the partition with a *Reader's Digest.* Guys like Joe and Sal had good intentions, and they liked my father. But after a few visits, they stopped coming. The Community Center, with the sauna and the familiar comradery, exerted its influence. Another Russian masseur had taken over my father's position and, although they swore he was "no Roman," it didn't help. After a short time, inconvenience superseded loyalty, and my father found himself staring at the walls.

Fearing just this sort of thing, my father had held on to his job at the chocolate bar factory. It was driving him crazy, but what was the alternative? To move from this factory job to another was pointless, and reapplying for welfare was out of the question. It had taken my parents two years to get on their feet and they were not prepared to face the implications of regression. So my father resolved to work five days at the factory and go to the office on weekends. As soon as he felt secure enough at the office he would abandon the factory and focus all of his attention on the business. The discussion was ongoing. To quit or not to quit. But as the original patients started to disappear, my father began to despair of ever being able to get out of the factory. None of this information, none of these discussions, were concealed from me. It seemed as though my parents had no secrets. I was nine, and there were many things I did not tell them, but there was nothing they would not openly discuss in front of me, often even soliciting my opinion. They were strangers in the country, and they recognized that the place was less strange to me, even though I was only a boy.

With the business grinding down to a state of terminal inertia, my father took the advice of some friends and went to seek the help of a certain rabbi. Others had gone to him before: Felix when he needed a job, Oleg for a good deal on a used car, and Robik and Eda for someone to cosign a loan. The rabbi was supposed to be particularly sympathetic to the plight of the Russian Jews. To improve his chances, my father brought me along.

To make me presentable to the rabbi, my mother ironed a pair of pants and put me into a clean golf shirt. My father and

I wore yarmulkes and walked hand in hand to the synagogue
not far from his office. It was rare for me to have this sort of
time with my father, as he was usually either working or ago-
nizing about not working. As we walked, I filled the silence
with the affairs of the third grade and my plans to make the
Selects team in the summer soccer league. It was a warm Sunday in June. To most of the people on the street—men on
their lawns, women with shopping bags, pensioners floating
by in their Buicks—we must have made a fine image. Father
and Son. Sunday stroll.

Seated across the table from the rabbi, my father wrestled
language and dignity to express need. I sat quietly beside him,
looking appropriately forlorn. I was sufficiently aware of our
predicament to feel the various permutations of shame: shame
for my father, shame for my shame, and even shame for the
rabbi, who seemed to be a decent guy. He was younger than
my father, and as if to compensate for his youth, he affected
a posture of liturgical gravity.

My father told the rabbi about his qualifications. He told
him about the years of training Olympic athletes to hoist almost inconceivable amounts of weight. He told him about
working as a masseur in the best sanatoriums along the Baltic
Sea. He told him about the months of study, his certificate
from the Board of Directors of Masseurs, the chocolate bar
factory, the one-room office, and the hard, hard work he was
willing to do. He also told him about Hebrew school and
what a good student I was. He encouraged the rabbi to speak
to me to see how well I'd learned the language. Slightly uncomfortable, the rabbi engaged me in a conversation in rudi-
mentary Hebrew.

—Do you like school?

—Yes, I like school.

—Do you like Canada?

—Yes, I like Canada.

My father, who could not follow the conversation, interrupted and told the rabbi that I could also sing Hebrew songs. The rabbi didn't seem particularly interested, but my father encouraged me out of my chair.

In the middle of the rabbi's office I stood and sang "Jerusalem of Gold." Halfway through the song I noticed the rabbi's attention flagging and I responded by trying to bring the song to a premature conclusion. The rabbi, visibly relieved, started to bring his hands together to create the first clap only to be reassured by my father that I was capable of singing more. To prove his point, my father poked me in the back, and I picked up the song where I'd happily abandoned it. The rabbi leaned forward, seemingly much more interested in my performance the second time around. When I was finally done, the rabbi gave me a five-dollar bill. For my father, he promised to spread the word about the business to his congregants. He also offered a word of advice: advertise.

Fifteen minutes after going in, we were back out on the street, hand in hand, and on our way home. For our trouble we had five dollars and the business card of a man who would print my father's flyers at cost.

The following week my father, mother, and I gathered around the kitchen table to compose the ideal advertisement for Roman's Therapeutic Massage. I was given the pen and assigned the responsibility of translating and transcribing my parents' concept for the flyer. My father wanted a strong emphasis placed on his experience with Olympic athletes, as it would provide prestige and imply familiarity with the human anatomy at the highest level. My mother, on the other hand, believed that his strongest selling point was his status as a Soviet refugee. The most important appeal, she said, was to guilt and empathy. That would get them in the door. Once they were in the door, then my father could impress them with his skill. In the end they agreed on a combination of the two. For my part, I contributed a list of familiar advertising superlatives.

Best New Therapeutic Massage Office!

Roman Berman, Soviet Olympic coach and refugee from Communist regime, provides Quality Therapeutic Massage Service!

Many years of experience in Special European techniques!

For all joint and muscle pain. Car accidents, work accidents, pregnancy, and general good physical conditioning.

Registered Massage Therapist. Office in convenient location and also visits to your house.

Satisfaction Guaranteed!

After the box of flyers arrived, my father and I loaded it into the trunk of the Pontiac and targeted the houses near the office. I took one side of the street, and my father took the other. To counteract my embarrassment, I made it a race: I would be the first to finish. I ran from house to house stuffing the flyers into mailboxes or handing them to people without making eye contact. Every now and again I would look across the street to gauge my father's progress. He was in no hurry. He wandered from house to house, going up the walkways, never stepping on the lawns. Whereas I tried to avoid people, my father lingered, passing deliberately in front of windows. Heeding my mother's instructions, he tried to be particularly conspicuous in front of homes with mezuzahs on the doorposts, hoping to catch sight of someone, to engage them in conversation. Most people weren't interested—except for one man who wanted to know how his own son could get a job delivering flyers.

With the flyers all gone, a new phase of waiting began. Now with every ring of the phone there was the potential for salvation. The phone existed like a new thing. From the moment we came home we were acutely conscious of it. It was either with us or against us. My father talked to it. As a sign of solidarity, I talked to it as well. When it was silent, my father would plead with it, curse it, threaten it. But when it rang, he would leap. He would come flying from the dinner table, the couch, the toilet. The phone would ring and he would leap. My mother would leap after him—her ear millimeters away from his exposed ear, listening, as if my father's head was itself the telephone. She listened as friends called, other friends called, my aunt called and called. Everybody called to see whether anybody had called.

By the time Dr. Kornblum called, an interminable week had passed. It was in the early afternoon and I was home alone. My mother would not be home for another hour, my father later still. When the phone rang I was already seated on the parquet floor in front of the television: I had a Hungarian salami sandwich on my lap as well as the plastic wrappers from a half dozen chocolate-covered prunes.

Kornblum told me I should call him Harvey. He was a doctor, he said, and he'd received my father's flyer and wanted to meet him. In fact, he wanted to meet the whole family.

How many of us were there—it didn't matter. We were all invited to his house for Friday night dinner. I should tell my parents that he would not take no for an answer. Kornblum with a K. Blum as in rhymes with room. As in there's plenty of room for everybody. Did I get all that? He gave me his phone number and told me to make sure my father gave him a call.

By the time my mother came home I was barely able to contain myself. I shared the good news and she overlooked the fact that I'd eaten the half dozen chocolate-covered prunes. I gave her the sheet of paper with Kornblum's name and telephone number and she quickly started dialing. My aunt was certain she had heard of this Kornblum before. When Victor Guttman's father slipped on the ice, wasn't it a Kornblum that did the operation? That Kornblum was very nice. Also very rich. It could be the same one. My mother called others. Sophatchka was studying to pass her medical boards and was familiar with many doctors. Did she know Kornblum? Kornblum the family physician or Kornblum the orthopedic surgeon? Not that it made a difference, they were both very successful. If either one referred even a small fraction of his patients our troubles would be over.

After washing his hands and changing out of his work jeans, my father crossed the room toward the phone. Merely crossing the room, he assumed a professional demeanor. With utmost solemnity he dialed Kornblum's number. My mother and I sat on the sofa and watched. She had already coached him on what to say. The goal was not to stray too far from the prepared script and to keep the phone call short and polite. God forbid he should say something wrong and upset Kornblum and then what would we do? My father dialed and all three of us waited as it rang. When someone answered, my father asked to speak with Dr. Kornblum. He waited again, apparently, for Kornblum to come to the phone. In the intervening silence my mother mouthed yet another reminder about how to behave. In response, my father turned his back on her and faced the wall. Moments passed before my father said that he was Roman Berman, massage therapist, and that he was returning Dr. Kornblum's call. Then he said, "Yes, okay, *Harvey.*"

Before Stalin, my great-grandmother lit the candles and made an apple cake every Friday night. In my grandfather's recollections of prewar Jewish Latvia, the candles and apple cakes feature prominently. When my mother was a girl, Stalin was already in charge, and although there was still apple cake, there were no more candles. By the time I was born, there were neither candles nor apple cake, though in my mother's mind, apple cake still meant Jewish. With this in mind, she retrieved the apple cake recipe and went to the expensive supermarket for the ingredients. And that Friday afternoon, she pleaded illness and left work early, coming home to bake so that the apple cake would be fresh for the Kornblums.

My father also left work early and drove to my school to pick me up. When we arrived home the apartment was redolent with the scent of apple cake. My mother hustled my father and me into the shower together so as not to waste time. I hadn't showered with my father in years and I didn't know where to look. My father, however, seemed oblivious to both his and my nudity. He soaped me up, rinsed me off, and put me into a towel. I stood on the bath mat watching through the glazed shower door as he hurriedly soaped his bald head and washed under his armpits. When he stepped out he looked surprised to find me still standing there.

Kornblum's turned out to be only a few streets away from my father's office. The house was on the left side of the street, which meant I had delivered Kornblum's flyer, but I didn't re-member it. My mother noted the size of the house. Maybe three thousand square feet with a big yard. Also, it was fully detached. This was two substantial steps beyond our means. Between our apartment and a fully detached house loomed the intermediate town house and the semidetached house. A fully detached house was the ultimate accomplishment. No-body we knew had even moved up to town house, though recently there had been plans and speculations.

Three abreast, we went up Kornblum's walk. My father was dressed in his blue Hungarian suit—veteran of interna-tional weightlifting competitions from Tallinn to Sochi. I had been put into a pair of gray trousers and a pressed white cot-ton shirt, with a silver Star of David on a silver chain not un-der but over the shirt. My mother wore a green wool dress that went nicely with her amber necklace, bracelet, and ear-rings. We were a sophisticated family—professional people with their straight-A-student son, future doctor or lawyer. With feigned confidence we strode up Kornblum's nicely trimmed walk: three refugees and a warm apple cake.

My father rang the bell. We heard footsteps. Then a man in slacks and a yellow sweater opened the door. The sweater had a little green alligator emblem on it. This was Kornblum. He was smiling broadly. He put a hand on my father's shoul-der and told us who we must be. My father must be Roman, my mother must be Bella, and I must be little Mark. He ush-ered us into the house. We followed him through the foyer and into the living room, where a table had been set. Six peo-ple were already seated around the table; three of the people were smiling like Kornblum. One of the smiling people was a woman who bustled over to my mother. Kornblum said this was his wife, Rhonda. Rhonda told us how nice it was that we could make it and relieved my mother of the apple cake. She told my mother she shouldn't have and took the apple cake into the kitchen.

Kornblum then introduced us to his good friends, the other two smiling people, Jerry Kogen and his wife, Shirley. Jerry and Shirley told us how wonderful it was to meet us. My mother said it was wonderful to meet them, too. My father nodded his head, smiled, and said thank you. He did this while glancing at the other three people at the table, the people who were not smiling like Kornblum, Rhonda, and their friends. A man, a woman, and a boy. Like us, they were over-dressed.

As Rhonda returned from the kitchen, Kornblum started to introduce us to the other family. Genady and Freda and their son, Simon, from Kharkov, wasn't that right? Genady said it was right. His English was a little better than my father's, but he had more gold teeth. In English, my mother told them how nice it was to meet them. In English, Freda thanked my mother. We were seated opposite them, and Jerry announced that Freda was also a medical professional—in Russia she had been a dentist. He himself was an eye doctor. Going around the table, they had most of the body covered. Eyes, teeth, Harvey with the bones, and Roman taking care of the muscles. What did that leave? Kornblum laughed and said he could think of a thing or two. Jerry laughed and Rhonda laughed and told Kornblum that he was too much. Genady and Freda laughed more than they needed to and so did my parents—though maybe a little less. Then Rhonda said a prayer and lit the candles.

Over roast chicken Kornblum told my parents and Genady and Freda what an honor it was to have them at his house. He could only imagine what they had gone through.

For years he and Rhonda had been involved with trying to help the Russian Jews. If it wasn't too personal, he wanted to know how bad it really was. My mother said it was bad, that the anti-Semitism was very bad. Jerry said that Genady and Freda had been refuseniks, he wanted to know if we had also been refuseniks. My mother hesitated a moment and then admitted that we had not been refuseniks. She knew some refuseniks, and we were almost refuseniks, but we were not refuseniks. Everyone agreed that this was very good, and then Freda and Genady told their story of being refuseniks. Midway through the story, the part where they have been evicted from their apartment and have to share a room with three other families, Genady lifted up his shirt to show everyone the place where he had been stabbed by former coworkers. He had a large scar below his ribs. Walking down the street one night, he stumbled upon some drunken comrades from the factory. They called him a filthy Jew traitor and the foreman went after him with a knife.

After Genady finished his story and tucked his shirt back into his pants, Jerry and Rhonda wiped tears from their eyes. They couldn't believe it was so horrible. My parents had to agree it was horrible. Kornblum said those Russian bastards and then asked if Simon and I wanted to go down to the basement and play. Kornblum's children, a boy and a girl, were away at sleepover camp. That was too bad. They would have been so excited to meet us. Downstairs in the basement was a Ping-Pong table, a pool table, a hockey net, and some other toys. As we went down, Freda was telling a story about her mother, who was stuck all alone in Kharkov. My parents weren't saying anything.

Aside from the Ping-Pong and pool tables, Kornblum's basement also had a big-screen television and a wall unit full of board games and books. In the corner, one of his kids had assembled the complete Star Wars Death Star. All the Star Wars figures were there including Ewoks. I went over to the Ping-Pong table. A paddle lay on top of a ball. I picked up the paddle and looked over at Simon. Simon didn't appear interested in Ping-Pong. He was inspecting the Death Star. In Russian, I asked him if all that stuff his father had said really happened. Are you calling my father a liar? he said, and picked up an R2-D2 doll. He picked up another toy and stuffed them both down his pants. What doesn't this rich bastard have, he said.

When I returned to the table everyone was there except my father and Rhonda. Shirley was sitting beside my mother admiring her amber necklace. Kornblum had a photo album out and was showing Genady and Freda pictures of his grandfather in Poland. Jerry also had a pile of old photographs on the table. On his father's side, his family was from Minsk. All the dinner plates had been cleared and there were now some pastries on the table and a pot of coffee. I had to go to the washroom and Kornblum said there was one downstairs and three upstairs, take your pick. He then turned a page in the album and pointed out everyone the Nazis had killed.

I went back through the foyer and looked for the washroom. The stairway leading up to the second floor was there so I climbed it. There was one bathroom in the hall but I heard voices from behind a door. The door led into the master bedroom, and the voices were coming from behind the door leading to the washroom. The door was partly open. Inside, Rhonda was sitting on a stool in front of the mirror, her blouse was undone and gathered at her waist. She was leaning forward on the bathroom counter in her bra and my father was massaging her neck. As I retreated, she called out and

pushed the door open with her foot. She said it was wonderful, my father was a magician, if only she could bottle his
hands and sell them. I mumbled that I had only been looking
for the washroom and she said that they were already finished.
She turned toward me and started doing up her blouse. Her
heavy breasts bulged over the top of her bra. She told me not
to worry, I should go ahead and do my business. Downstairs
Harvey was probably waiting for her to make more coffee.

As my father washed the Vaseline lotion from his hands, I
stood in front of the toilet with my pants undone. He dried
his hands on the decorator towels and waited for me to pee.
After a while he asked if I wanted him to wait outside. After a
little while longer he left and waited in the bedroom. When I
came out my father was sitting on Kornblum's bed. Above
him was a large family portrait taken for Kornblum's daughter's bat mitzvah. The Kornblums, formally dressed, were
seated on the grass under a large tree. My father wasn't looking
at the portrait. He said, Tell me, what am I supposed to do?
Then he got up, took my hand, and we went back downstairs.

At the table everyone was eating pastries. Shirley was still
sitting beside my mother. She was trying on my mother's amber bracelet. As my father came in she shuffled over to make
room for us. Rhonda announced that my father was a miracle
worker. Her neck had never felt better. She made Kornblum
promise to send him some of his patients. Kornblum said it
would be an honor. Kornblum said my father would get a call
Monday morning. Before he knew it, he would be out of
the chocolate bar factory. Kornblum would spread the word.
A chocolate bar factory was no place for a man like my
father. Jerry said that my father could count on him to help in
any way.

On our way out Kornblum shook hands with my father,

and with me, and then he kissed my mother on the cheek. It had been a very special evening for him and Rhonda. Rhonda came out of the kitchen carrying my mother's apple cake. She didn't want it to go to waste. Even though they sometimes took the kids to McDonald's, they kept kosher at home. So although it smelled wonderful, unfortunately they couldn't keep it.

As we walked back to the Pontiac it was unclear whether nothing or everything had changed. We returned much as we came, the only tangible evidence of the passage of time was the cold apple cake. Before us was the Pontiac, as green and ugly as ever. Behind us was Kornblum's fully detached house. We walked slowly, in no hurry to reach our destination. Somewhere between Kornblum's and the Pontiac was our fate. It floated above us like an ether, ambiguous and perceptible.

My father stopped walking. He contemplated my mother and the apple cake.

—Why are you still carrying it?

—What am I supposed to do?

—Throw it away.

—Throw it away? It's a shame to waste it.

—Throw it away. It's bad luck.

Something in the way my mother balked confirmed my own suspicion. There were countless superstitions, numberless ways of inviting calamity, but I had never heard anything about disposing of an unwanted cake. Also, my mother had worked hard on the cake. The ingredients had cost money, and she abhorred the idea of wasting food. Still, she didn't argue. Nothing was certain. We needed luck and were susceptible to the wildest irrationality. Rightly or wrongly, the cake was now tainted. My mother handed it to me and pointed down the street toward a Dumpster.

She did not need to say run.

THE SECOND STRONGEST MAN

I N THE WINTER OF 1984, as my mother was recovering from a nervous breakdown and my father's business hovered precipitously between failure and near failure, the international weightlifting championships were held at the Toronto Convention Centre. One evening the phone rang and a man invited my father to serve on the panel of judges. The job paid next to nothing but my father took it for the sake of his dignity. If only for a few days, he would wear his old IWF blazer and be something other than a struggling massage therapist and schlepper of chocolate bars. In the bedroom my father retrieved a passport with his International Weightlifting Federation credentials. The passport contained a photo of him taken years before the trials of immigration. In the picture his face carried the detached confidence of the highly placed Soviet functionary. I had seen the picture many times, and occasionally, when my father wasn't home, I took it out and studied it. It was comforting to think that the man in the picture and my father were once the same person.

Several days after the phone call we received an official package from the IWF. I joined my parents at the kitchen table and scanned through the list of competitors. There, as part of the Soviet delegation, were the names Sergei Federenko and Gregory Ziskin. My mother asked my father what this meant. Did it mean we would get to see them? Did it mean they would see our apartment? It had been little more than a week since the last time the paramedics had come, wrapped my mother in an orange blanket, strapped her to a gurney, and taken her to Branson Hospital. For months she had been stricken with paralyzing anxiety and a lethargy that made it impossible for her to undertake even the most basic household tasks. These had been months of boiled eggs, Lipton chicken noodle soup, an accumulation of sticky patches on the kitchen floor, and dust in the corners. My God, Sergei can't see the apartment like this, she said.

I sprang up from the table, unable to restrain my enthusiasm. I pranced around the apartment singing, Seryozha, Seryozha, Seryozha. Seryozha is coming!

My father told me to be quiet already.

—Seryozha, Seryozha, Seryozha.

My mother got up and handed me the broom.

—If you can't sit still, start sweeping.

—Seryozha is coming, I sang to the broom.

Five years before we left Latvia my father operated a very successful side venture out of the gym at Riga Dynamo. At that time he was one of the head administrators at Dynamo and was responsible for paper shuffling and budget manipulation. Before that he had been a very good varsity athlete and an accomplished coach of the VEF radio factory's soccer team. For a Jew, he was well liked by his superiors, and so they turned a blind eye when he and Gregory Ziskin—a fellow administrator and Jew—started their bodybuilding program in the evenings. At best, the directors hoped that the class would lead to the discovery of a new lifter; at worst, it meant they would get a piece of the action.

Every Monday, Wednesday, and Friday from six to nine my father and Gregory unlocked the back door of the Dynamo gym and admitted their eager bodybuilders. Most of these were Jewish university students and young professionals who wanted to look good on the beaches of Jurmala. They were hardly inspired athletes but they came regularly and were pleased with their results. My father and Gregory assigned routines and oversaw their exercises. For my father the class was a welcome break from the obligations of Soviet bureaucracy—the endless documents, detailed reports, and formal presentations to the Dynamo directors and visiting dignitaries. Also, the money was good. After kickbacks to the Dynamo directors and a few rubles to the janitor, my father and Gregory each pocketed thirty extra rubles a month—more than double the rent on our three-room apartment.

My father and Gregory ran the class for several years without incident. The directors received their cut and kept quiet. As long as the Dynamo teams were placing well, nobody was willing to mess with a good thing, and at the time, Riga Dynamo was clicking along: Victor Tikhonov worked magic with the hockey team before being promoted to Moscow and Red Army; Ivanchenko became the first middleweight to lift a combined 500 kilos; and the basketball and volleyball teams were feared across Europe. So nobody paid much attention to my father's class.

It was only in the mid-1970s that things started to turn. As Jews began to emigrate many of my father's bodybuilders requested visas to Israel. Dynamo represented the KGB and someone at the ministry started making connections. It was pointed out to one of my father's directors that there was a disturbing correlation between my father's bodybuilders and Jews asking for exit visas. My father and Gregory were invited into the director's office and informed of the suspicions. These were the sorts of suspicions that could get them all into trouble. It wouldn't look good at all if the Riga Dynamo gym was sponsoring anti-Soviet activities. The director, an old friend, asked my father whether the bodybuilding class was a front for Zionist agitation. It was an unpleasant conversation, but everyone understood that this could only be the beginning of the unpleasantness. The class was now being closely monitored. The only way to keep from shutting it down would be to justify its existence in an official capacity. In other words, they had better discover some talent.

After the meeting with the director, my father suggested to Gregory that the smart thing to do would be to end the class. They'd made their money, and since my parents had already resolved to leave the Soviet Union, this was exactly the sort of incident that could create serious problems. Gregory, who had no plans to emigrate, but who also had no interest in a trip to Siberia, agreed. They decided not to continue the class beyond the end of the month.

The following day my father discovered Sergei Federenko.

On the night my father discovered Sergei Federenko the class ended later than usual. Gregory left early and my father remained with five students. It was almost ten when my father opened the back door of the gym and stepped out into the alley where three young soldiers were singing drunken songs. The smallest of the three was pissing against the wall. My father turned in the opposite direction, but one of his students decided to flex his new muscles. He accused the little soldier of uncivilized behavior, called him a dog, and said unflattering things about his mother.

The little soldier continued pissing as if nothing had happened, but the two bigger soldiers got ready to crack skulls.

—Would you listen to Chaim? A real tough Jew bastard.

—You apologize, Chaim, before it's too late.

My father envisioned a catastrophe. Even if by some miracle he and his students weren't killed, the police would get involved. The consequences of police involvement would be worse than any beating.

Before his student could respond, my father played the conciliator. He apologized for the student. He explained that he was part of a bodybuilding class. His head was still full of adrenaline. He didn't know what he was saying. Doctors had proven that as muscles grow the brain shrinks. He didn't want any trouble. They should accept his apology and forget the whole thing.

As my father spoke the little soldier finished pissing on the wall and buttoned up his trousers. Unlike his two friends, he was completely unperturbed. He reached into his pants pocket and retrieved a small bottle of vodka. One of the other soldiers pointed to a black Moskvich sedan parked in the alley.

—Listen, faggot, if one of your boys can lift the Moskvich we'll forget the whole thing.

They made a deal. The Moskvich had to be lifted from the back and held at least a meter off the ground. Even though the engine was at the front, the back of the car was sufficiently heavy. Taking into account the frame, wheels, tires, and whatever might be kept in the trunk, the total would be in the hundreds of pounds. Maybe three hundred? Maybe four? It was an impossible bet. None of his students would be able to do it. It would be an exercise in futility. They would certainly be humiliated, but from my father's perspective, humiliation was better than a beating and a police inquiry. So, out of respect for my father, his students shut up and endured the ridicule. One by one they squatted under the car's bumper.

—Careful, Chaim, don't shit your pants.

—Lift it for Mother Russia.

—Lift it for Israel.

As expected, none of them could so much as get it off the ground. When they were done, one of the soldiers turned to the student who had started the trouble.

—Not so tough now, Chaim?

—It's impossible.

—Impossible for Chaim.

—Impossible even for a stupid cocksucker like you.

Amazingly, instead of killing the student, the big soldier turned to the little soldier.

—Sergei, show Chaim what's impossible.

The little soldier put his bottle back into his pocket and walked over to the Moskvich.

—Chaim, you watch the stupid cocksucker.

Sergei squatted under the bumper, took a deep breath, and lifted the car a meter off the ground.

From the time I was four until we left Riga two years later, Sergei was a regular visitor to our apartment on Kasmonaftikas. As a rule, he would come and see us whenever he returned from an international competition. Two years after my father discovered him, Sergei was a member of the national team, had attained the prestigious title of "International Master of Sport," and possessed all three world records in his weight class. My father called him the greatest natural lifter he had ever seen. He was blessed with an economy of movement and an intuition for the mechanics of lifting. He loved to lift the way other people love drugs or chocolate. Growing up on a kolkhoz, he had been doing a man's work since the age of twelve. Life had consisted of hauling manure, bailing hay, harvesting turnips, and lugging bulky farm equipment. When the army took him at eighteen he had never been more than thirty kilometers from the kolkhoz. Once he left he never intended to return. His father was an alcoholic and his mother had died in an accident when he was three. His gratitude to my father for rescuing him from the army and the kolkhoz was absolute. As he rose through the ranks, his loyalty remained filial and undiminished. And in 1979, when we left Riga, Sergei was as devoted to my father as ever. By then he could no longer walk down the street without being approached by strangers. In Latvia, he was as recognizable as any movie star. Newspapers in many countries called him, pound for pound, the strongest man in the world.

Sergei left a deep impression on my four-, five-, and six-year-old mind. There wasn't much I remembered from Riga—isolated episodes, little more than vignettes, mental artifacts—but many of these recollections involved Sergei. My memories, largely indistinct from my parents' stories, constituted my idea of Sergei. A spectrum inverted through a prism, stories and memories refracted to create the whole: Sergei as he appeared when he visited our apartment on Kasmonaftikas. Dressed in the newest imported fashions, he brought exotic gifts: pineapples, French perfume, Swiss chocolate, Italian sunglasses. He told us about strange lands where everything was different—different trains, different houses, different toilets, different cars. Sometimes he arrived alone, other times he was accompanied by one of the many pretty girls he was dating. When Sergei visited I was spastic with a compulsion to please him. I shadowed him around the apartment, I swung from his biceps like a monkey, I did somersaults on the carpet. The only way I could be convinced to go to sleep was if Sergei followed my mother into my bedroom. We developed a routine. Once I was under the covers Sergei said good night by lifting me and my little bed off the floor. He lifted the bed as though it weighed no more than a newspaper or a sandwich. He raised me to his chest and wouldn't put me back down until I named the world's strongest man.

—Seryozha, Seryozha Federenko!

My father took me with him to the Sutton Place Hotel where the Soviet delegation had their rooms. A KGB agent always traveled with the team, but it turned out that my father knew him. My father had met him on the two or three occasions when he had toured with Dynamo through Eastern Europe. The agent was surprised to see my father.

—Roman Abramovich, you're here? I didn't see you on the plane.

My father explained that he hadn't taken the plane. He lived here now. A sweep of my father's arm defined "here" broadly. The sweep included me. My jacket, sneakers, and Levi's were evidence. Roman Abramovich and his kid lived here. The KGB agent took an appreciative glance at me. He nodded his head.

—You're living well?

—I can't complain.

—It's a beautiful country. Clean cities. Big forests. Nice cars. I also hear you have good dentists.

In the hotel lobby, the KGB agent opened his mouth and showed my father the horrific swelling around a molar. He had been in agony for weeks. In Moscow, a dentist had extracted a neighboring tooth and the wound had become infected. On the plane, with the cabin pressure, he had thought he would go insane. Eating was out of the question and sleep was impossible without 1,000 grams of vodka, minimum. But he couldn't very well do his job if he was drunk all the time. Also, he'd been told that vodka was very expensive here. What he needed was a dentist. If my father could arrange for a Toronto dentist to help him he would owe him his life. The pain was already making him think dark thoughts. In his room on the twenty-eighth floor he had stood at the window and considered jumping.

Using the hotel phone, my father called Dusa, our dentist. A top professional in Moscow, she had not yet passed her Canadian exams. In the interim, she worked nights as a maid for a Canadian dentist with whom she had an informal arrangement which allowed her to use his office to see her own patients, for cash, under the table. The Canadian dentist got fifty percent with the understanding that in the event of trouble, he would deny everything and it would be Dusa's ass on the line. Fortunately, after months and months of work, there had been no trouble. And several times a week, after she finished cleaning the office, Dusa saw her motley assortment of patients. All of them Russian immigrants without dental insurance. My father explained this to the KGB officer and told him that if he wasn't averse to seeing a dentist at one in the morning, he had himself an appointment.

As a token of his gratitude, the KGB agent personally escorted us up to Sergei's room. So long as Sergei appeared at the competition and was on the flight to Moscow with the rest of the team, everything else was of no consequence. We could see him as much as we liked. The KGB agent swore on his children's eyes that there would be no problems.

At Sergei's door, the agent knocked sharply.

—Comrade Federenko, you have important visitors!

Dressed in official gray slacks and buttoning his shirt, Sergei opened the door. He hesitated to speak until the KGB agent slapped my father's back and confessed that he was always deeply moved to witness a reunion of old friends. Then, Dusa's address in his pocket, he turned and departed down the carpeted hall.

In the hallway, Sergei embraced my father and kissed him in the Soviet style. Next to Sergei, my father—five feet six and 170 pounds—looked big. I hadn't expected the physical Sergei to be so small—even though I had memorized his records the way American kids memorized box scores and knew that he was in the lowest weight class at 52 kilos.

—That bastard, he scared the hell out of me.

—The KGB, they know how to knock on a door.

—Especially that one. A true Soviet patriot.

Sergei looked down the hall in the direction of the KGB agent's departure. My father looked. So did I. The man had gone.

Sergei turned back, looked at my father, and grinned.

—I was in the washroom, I almost pissed myself. I thought, if I'm lucky, it's only another drug test.

—Since when are you afraid of drug tests?

—Since never.

—Do I need to remind you of our regard for drug tests?

In his capacity as Dynamo administrator it had been my father's responsibility to ensure that all the weightlifters were taking their steroids. At the beginning of each week he handed out the pills along with the special food coupons. Everyone knew the drill: no pills, no food.

—Absolutely not. Keeps the sport clean.

—And, of course, you're clean.

—I'm clean. The team is clean. Everyone is clean.

—Good to hear nothing has changed.

—Nothing.

Sergei clapped my father on the shoulder.

—What a wonderful surprise.

On our way to the hotel, I had been rabid with excitement to see Sergei, but seeing him in person, I couldn't speak. I stood behind my father and waited to be acknowledged. It seemed like a very long time before Sergei turned his attention to me. When he finally did, he looked down and appeared not to know me.

—And who is this?

—You don't recognize him?

—He looks familiar.

—Think.

—It's hard to say.

—Take a guess.

—Well, if I had to guess, I would say he looks a little like Mark. But he's too small.

—Too small?

—Mark was much bigger. He could do fifteen, maybe even twenty push-ups. This one looks like he couldn't even do ten.

—I can do twenty-five! I do them every morning.

—I don't believe it.

I dropped down onto the red and gold Sutton Place carpet and Sergei counted them from one to twenty-five. Panting, I got back up and waited for Sergei's reaction. He smiled and spread his arms.

—Come on, boy, jump.

I leapt. Sergei carried me into the hotel room and I hung

from his arm as my father called Gregory's room. Sergei's competition was two days away and it was decided that he would spend a little time with us the next day and then he and Gregory would come for dinner after his competition.

When my father and I returned from the hotel with the good news, my mother was scrubbing every available surface. Floors, oven, furniture, windows. She presented us with several bags of garbage which we dropped down the smelly chute in the hallway. My father told her that Sergei looked good. As though he hadn't changed at all in the last five years.

—What did he say about the way you look?

—He said I looked good. Canadian. Younger than the last time he saw me.

—If you look young, then I must be a schoolgirl.

—You are a schoolgirl.

—The ambulance comes once a week. Some schoolgirl.

The next morning my father stopped at the hotel on his way to judge events in the middleweight class. Sergei wasn't competing that day and I took the subway with my father so that I could guide Sergei back to our apartment, where my mother was waiting to take him shopping. As we crossed the lobby toward the elevator I noticed the KGB agent making his way over to intercept us. I noticed before my father noticed. From a distance I had the vague impression that there was something not quite the same about the agent. As he drew closer I saw that his face was badly swollen. With every step he took the swelling became more prominent. It was as though the swelling preceded his face. From a distance he had been arms, legs, torso, haircut, but up close he was a swollen jaw. My father, distracted by his obligations to the competition and nervous about being late, didn't appear to recognize the man until he was standing directly in front of him. But then, on seeing the agent's face, my father stiffened and seized me by the shoulder. My God, he said, and simultaneously drew me back, putting himself between me and the KGB agent.

The KGB agent clapped his hands and broke into what appeared to be a lopsided grin. His distended lips barely parted but parted enough to reveal white cotton gauze clamped between his teeth. When he spoke, it was through this gruesome leer, like a man with his jaw wired shut. My father tightened his grip on the back of my neck.

—Roman Abramovich, looks like you really did me a favor.

—She's the dentist for my family. I go to her. My wife. My son. I swear she always does good work.

The agent's jaw muscles twitched as he clamped tighter into his grin.

—Good work. Look at me. I couldn't ask for better. She put in three crowns and a bridge.

—She's a very generous woman.

—She knows how to treat a man. Anesthetic and a bottle of vodka. I left at four in the morning. A very generous woman. And beautiful. It was a wonderful night, you understand.

—I'm glad to hear you're happy.

—Roman Abramovich, remember, you always have a friend in Moscow. Visit anytime.

Laughing at his joke, the agent turned, and we proceeded to the elevator and rode up to Sergei's floor. In the elevator my father leaned against the wall and finally loosened his grip on my neck.

—Don't ever forget. This is why we left. So you never have to know people like him.

We knocked on Sergei's door, and after some shuffling, Sergei answered. He was in the middle of his push-ups when he let us into his room. He was wearing an undershirt and his arms were a bold relief of muscles, tendons, and veins. In Italy, during our six-month purgatory between Russia and Canada, I had seen statues with such arms. I understood that the statues were meant to reflect the real arms of real men, but except for Sergei I had never met anyone with arms like that.

As my father was in a hurry, he left me with Sergei as he rushed back out to the convention center. I waited while Sergei dressed.

—So where are you taking me today?

—Mama says we'll go to the supermarket. She thinks you'll like it.

—The supermarket.

—The good supermarket. They have every kind of food.

—And you know how to get there?

—Yes. First we take the subway and then the bus. By the subway and the bus I know how to go almost anywhere.

—How about California?

—The subway doesn't go to California.

—Then maybe we should take a plane.

The way he said it I didn't know if he was joking or serious until he laughed. I wanted to laugh too but I hadn't understood the joke. I sensed that I wasn't intended to understand it in the first place. I was hurt because I wanted very much to be Sergei's equal, his friend, and I suspected that Sergei wasn't laughing at his joke but rather at me.

Seeing that he had upset me, Sergei tried to make up for it by asking about the supermarket.

—We sometimes go to another one that isn't as good. In the other one they don't have the things they show on the television. But at the good supermarket you can find everything.

On the bus ride home I pointed out the landmarks that delineated our new life. To compensate for the drabness of the landscape I animated my hands and voice. I felt the tour guide's responsibility to show Sergei something interesting. At the northern edge of the city, home to Russian immigrants, brown apartment buildings, and aging strip malls, there wasn't much to show. I stressed our personal connection to each mundane thing, hoping in that way to justify its inclusion. There was the Canadian Tire store where I got my bicycle, the Russian Riviera banquet hall where my father celebrated his birthday, one delicatessen called Volga and another called Odessa, a convenience store where I played video games, my school, my hockey arena, my soccer fields. Sergei looked and nodded. I kept talking and talking even though I could tell that what I was showing and what he was seeing were not the same things.

When the bus pulled up near our apartment building I was relieved to stop talking. Sergei followed me into the lobby. I used my key and let us inside. Upstairs, my mother was waiting. For the first time in months she was wearing makeup and what appeared to be a new dress. In the dining room there was a vase with flowers. There was a bowl on the coffee table with yellow grapes. There was another bowl beside it containing assorted Russian bonbons: Karakum, Brown Squirrel, Clumsy Bear. When my mother saw Sergei, her face lit up with true happiness. Involuntarily, I looked away. After so many miserable months I was surprised by my reaction. I had been praying for her to get better, but there was something about the pitch of her happiness that made me feel strangely indecent. I had felt this way once before when I accidentally glimpsed her undressing through a doctor's office door. Here as there, instinct proscribed against looking at my mother's nakedness.

From our apartment my mother drove our green Pontiac to the good supermarket and then the mall where Sergei bought blue jeans for himself and for the woman he was dating. Also, on my recommendation, he bought some shirts with the Polo logo on them which were very popular at the time. Against my mother's protestations he also insisted on buying a shirt for me and one for my father.

—Bellachka, don't forget, you wake up in the morning, you get into your car, you go to a store, you can buy anything you want. In Riga people now line up just for permission to line up.

I was grateful when my mother didn't say anything to contradict him, since both she and I knew that the only way we could afford fifty-dollar shirts was if Sergei paid for them.

When my father returned from the convention center that night he was exhilarated. He had witnessed two world records. One by a Soviet lifter he had known. He was energized by the proximity to his former life. He had seen old friends. People recognized him. He had also spent a few hours with Gregory Ziskin and they had been able to have a drink in Gregory's hotel room. Gregory had filled him in on the Dynamo gossip. Colleagues who had received promotions, others who had retired. The politics with directors. New athletes on the rise. Gregory was proud that, including Sergei, the national team had three weightlifters from Riga Dynamo. There was a new young lifter named Krutov in Sergei's weight class who showed considerable promise. He had been taking silver behind Sergei for the past year. Having the gold and silver medalists was doing wonders for Gregory's profile with the ministry. He'd heard rumors of a transfer to Moscow and a permanent position with Red Army.

As a souvenir, my father surprised me with a poster signed by the Soviet national team. We, in turn, surprised him with his Polo shirt. In the living room, my father and I tried on our new shirts. My father said he couldn't think of when he would wear it. He had plenty of shirts. I had plenty of shirts too, but I felt as though I had only one.

Along with the poster my father also secured tickets for me and my mother for the next day's competition. My mother, anxious about preparing dinner, felt she couldn't go. Even though she wanted very much to see Sergei compete. I had no obligations. The competition was on a Saturday. I had no school, no homework. Nothing that could keep me from watching Sergei perform.

At the convention center dozens of wooden risers had been joined together to create a stage. At one edge of the stage was a long table for the officials. My father had his place there along with the two other judges. A small black electrical box sat squarely in front of each judge. The box was connected by wires to a display board. On the box were two buttons, one button for a good lift, the second button for failure. Before the competition started my father allowed me to sit in his seat and press the buttons. As I sat there Gregory Ziskin approached. I had only faint memories of Gregory, who, unlike Sergei, hadn't often come to the apartment. He was my father's friend and business partner, but there was a quality to his demeanor that stressed the professional over the personal. He looked perpetually impatient.

At my father's suggestion Gregory agreed to take me behind the stage so I could watch the lifters warming up. In Riga it was something my father had enjoyed doing. He always liked the energy of the warm-up room. But now, as a judge, it was unacceptable for him to give even the impression of bias or impropriety. Leaving my father to review papers, I followed Gregory through a heavy curtain toward the sounds of grunting and clanging iron.

Standing in the wings, I watched a scene I recognized as familiar only once I saw it. The warm-up room was very big, the size of a high school gymnasium. There was activity everywhere. In small groups, coaches and trainers attended to their athletes. Teams could be distinguished from one another by the colors of their Adidas training suits. Some of the lifters wore the suits, others had stripped down to their tights. In one corner I watched as trainers wrapped and taped knees, in another corner other trainers had set up massage tables. In the center of the room a large section of the floor had been covered with plywood. Several bars had been set up for the lifters. There were also chalk caddies. I looked on with fascination as the men went through their rituals of applying the chalk to their hands, arms, and shoulders. To handle the perfect white cakes of chalk seemed reason enough to become a weightlifter.

Gregory, who had important matters to attend to, left me with a plastic press pass and instructions not to get into any trouble. I could stick around as long as I liked, or at least until

someone told me to leave. I watched him head over to the Soviet delegation, where Sergei was stretching beside a young
blond weightlifter. From every corner came the sounds of exer-
tion, of metal striking metal and metal striking wood. Nobody
paid me any attention as I wandered around. I finally took up
a position near the center of the room and watched men lift
heavy things in preparation for lifting very heavy things.

The competition took hours. My father reserved me a seat in
the front so that my view wouldn't be obscured by the heads
of adults. Sergei's weight class was one of the last on the sched-
ule. Until Sergei performed I spent most of my time watching
my father. Up onstage with the other judges, he looked very
much like his old picture in the IWF passport.

Sergei's weight class competed in the afternoon. Very
quickly it became clear that it was a competition between two
men: Sergei and Krutov, the blond weightlifter. Their first lifts
exceeded those of the rest of the competitors by several kilos.
After that, from attempt to attempt, they performed only
against each other. I watched first as Sergei eclipsed his world
record in the snatch and then as Krutov matched it. Each one
lifting fluidly, in one motion, almost twice his own weight.

When it came time for the clean and jerk Sergei declined
the opening weight and watched as Krutov successfully approached and then matched Sergei's world record. To catch
Krutov, Sergei had three attempts. During Sergei's lifts, Krutov waited silently in the wings. I sat on my hands and
watched as Sergei failed on his first attempt, and then, minutes later, on his second. Both times, straining under the bar,
he managed to get the weight up to his chest and no farther.
Until Sergei's final lift, it hadn't occurred to me that he could

lose. But as he chalked his hands in preparation for the lift, it not only occurred to me that he might lose, but, all at once, I knew he would. I looked at the people around me and sensed that they also knew it. Sergei seemed to know it too. He paced the stage almost until his time expired. I watched the seconds on the huge clock behind him tick away. Just to stay in the competition, he had to match his own world record. And when he failed to do it, when he was unable to steady the bar above his head, when all three judges' lights—including my father's—glowed red, I felt sick. As I watched Sergei embrace Krutov and then Krutov embrace Gregory, I tasted and then swallowed the eggs I had eaten for breakfast.

After the awards ceremony I followed my father over to Sergei. He was standing slightly apart from Gregory, Krutov, and the rest of the Soviet team. When he saw us he forced a smile. My father congratulated him and Sergei held up his silver medal. He took it off his neck and let me hold it. He kept the smile on his face.

—A silver medal. It's not gold, but I guess you don't find them lying in the street.

Sergei looked over to where Gregory was standing with his arm around Krutov.

—Don't forget to congratulate Comrade Ziskin on another great day for Dynamo. Another one-two finish. What difference does it make to him if all of a sudden one is two and two is one?

At home, my mother had prepared a large and elaborate dinner. There were salads, a cold borscht, smoked pike, smoked whitefish, a veal roast, and tea, cake, and ice cream for dessert. She had set the table for five and used crystal glasses and her good china. I wore my clean new Polo shirt. My father told amusing stories about our immigration in Italy. He made an effort to reminisce with Gregory about their old bodybuilding students. The ones who remained in Riga, those who were now in Toronto, others who sometimes wrote letters from New York and Israel. My mother inquired after some of her girlfriends. People in the Jewish community whom Gregory would have known even though he and my mother were almost a generation apart. Even I talked about what my school was like, what sorts of cars my Hebrew school friends had. The only person who didn't talk was Sergei. He listened to all the conversations and drank. My father had placed a bottle of vodka on the table, and after the requisite toasts, only Sergei continued to address the bottle. With the bottle almost gone, he suddenly turned on Gregory and accused him of plotting against him. He knew that Gregory planned to recommend that he be removed from the team.

—He wants to put me out to pasture. Soviet pasture. The rest of my life grazing in the dust. The only way he'll get me back there is with a bullet through my head.

Sergei kept drinking, even though it looked like he was having a hard time keeping his eyes open.

—Roman, you did the right thing. You got the hell out of that cemetery. Now you can look forward to a real life. And what do we look forward to? What kind of life, Gregory Davidovich, you KGB cocksucker!

After another drink Sergei's head began to drift toward his plate and he accepted my father's help and rose from the table. His arm draped over my father's shoulder, Sergei stumbled into my bedroom and onto my single bed. My father closed the door and returned to the table. He lowered himself wearily into his chair. Submitting to gravity, he looked again like my old father.

As my mother served the tea Gregory confessed that Sergei was more right than wrong. But this was something my father knew as well as he did. A weightlifter's career was five, maybe seven years. After that there was a nice arrangement. A position with Dynamo. A lucrative job with customs. Maybe a coaching placement, or moving papers from one corner of the desk to the other. Sergei would get what everyone else got. He'd keep his three-room apartment, he'd have his garage for his car, he'd never have to worry about a salary. That Russia was becoming a colossal piece of shit was a different story. That my father had proven himself a genius by leaving was undeniable. Dunking biscuits into his tea, Gregory admitted he should have left when he had the chance. Now it was too late.

My father looked at my mother before speaking.

—Don't be fooled, Grisha. I often think of going back.

—Are you insane? Look at what you have. Take a walk outside. I saw beggars on the street wearing Levi's jeans and Adidas running shoes.

—Three days out of five I'm afraid I'll join them.

—Roma, come on, I've known you for thirty years. You don't have to lie on my account.

—I'm not lying. Every day is a struggle.

—Look, I'm not blind. I see your car. I see your apartment. I see how you struggle. Believe me, your worst day is better than my best.

Leaving my parents and Gregory at the table, I went down the hall and into my bedroom. Even though I knew every step blind, I waited for my eyes to become accustomed to the dark. Sergei was stretched out on my single bed, his feet barely hanging over the edge. I went over and stood beside him. I listened to his breathing and considered his body through his suit jacket. Again, I was amazed at how small he was. I bent closer to examine his face. I didn't mind that he was in my bed, although I wondered where I would sleep if he stayed. When he suddenly opened his eyes, I was startled.

—Well, boy, what do you see?

He raised himself to a sitting position and looked me over. He put his hands on my shoulders and my arms and gripped for a proper appraisal.

—How many push-ups can you do?

—Twenty-five.

—Only twenty-five?

—I think so.

—For a boy like you, anything less than fifty is a disgrace.

He climbed off the bed and kneeled on the floor. He patted a spot beside him.

—Come on, come on.

When I hesitated his hand shot up and seized me by my new Polo shirt. I felt the fabric tear and heard two buttons strike the floor.

—Let's go. You and me. Fifty push-ups.

At first I managed to keep up with him, but after a while he began to race ahead. I strained not to fall behind, afraid of what he might do to me. But he continued to do the exercise, counting to himself, not minding me at all. When he finished I finished as well.

—See, it feels good.

I nodded my head in agreement.

Sergei looked over at my alarm clock. It read past ten.

—Look at how late it is. Shouldn't you be asleep?

—It's okay. Sometimes I stay up until eleven.

—When you were in Riga it was nine o'clock sharp. You remember how you liked it when I used to put you to sleep?

—I remember.

—It wasn't so long ago.

—No.

—Come on, into bed.

—It's okay. I don't really have to.

—Into bed. Into bed.

His tone left no room for negotiation. I kicked off my shoes and lifted the covers.

—Good.

Sergei knelt down beside my bed and gripped the wooden frame.

—Comfortable?

—Yes.

His face straining, he used his legs and rose from the floor; my bed resisting, scratching the wall, but leaving the ground. At first the bed tottered and I gripped the sides, but then he steadied it. Smiling triumphantly, he looked at me. I heard the door opening behind him. I recognized my father's footsteps. Then other footsteps. My mother's. Gregory's.

—Nu, boy, tell me. Who is the world's strongest man?

Looking past Sergei at my father, I waited to see if he was going to do something. My mother started to take a step forward but my father restrained her.

—Nu, boy? Who is the world's strongest man?

—Seryozha. Seryozha Federenko.

—Wrong, boy. That was yesterday's answer.

He laughed and turned to face Gregory.

—Isn't that right Gregory Davidovich?

—Put him down, you idiot.

Seryozha emitted something that was a cross between a cough and a laugh. He carefully eased my bed to the ground and proceeded to slump down on the floor. Gregory and my father both moved to help him up, but as Gregory reached for his arm Sergei violently slapped it aside.

—You bastard, don't you dare put a hand on me.

Gregory stepped back. My father carefully took hold of Sergei's armpits and helped him up. Without protesting, Sergei put his arms across my father's shoulders.

—Roman, you were the only one who gave a shit about me, and we will never see each other again.

With faltering steps, my father supported Sergei into the hall. I got out of my bed and stood in my doorway. Gregory followed my father and Sergei into the hall and toward the front door. My mother came over and stood with me.

My father offered to drive or call them a cab.

Gregory shook his head and smiled the familiar Soviet smile.

—What for? Have you forgotten? There is always a car waiting downstairs.

Still holding on to my father, Sergei permitted himself to be led down the hall and into the elevator. Gregory said good-bye to my mother as she closed the door behind him. I went to my bedroom window and waited. Below, in the parking lot, I saw a man smoking beside a dark sedan. In slightly more than the amount of time it took for the elevator to descend to the lobby, my father appeared in the parking lot with Sergei clinging to his shoulders. Gregory followed. The man opened the rear door and my father eased Sergei into the car. I watched as my father shook hands with Gregory and with the man. As my father turned back in the direction of our building the man opened the driver's-side door. For an instant, the light from the car's interior was sufficient to illuminate his swollen face.

AN ANIMAL TO THE MEMORY

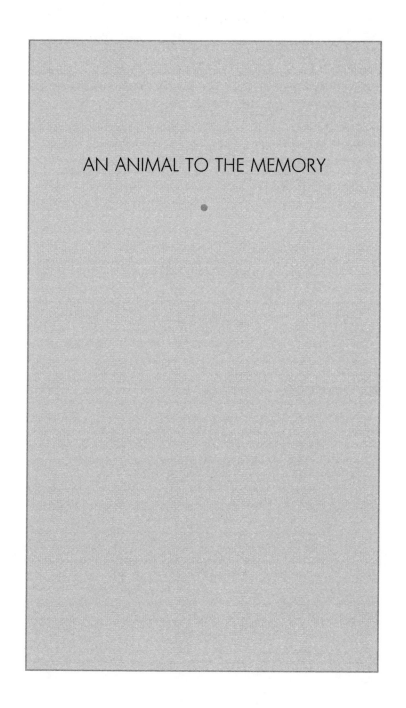

O N THE RAILWAY PLATFORM in Vienna, my mother and aunt forbade my cousin and me from saying goodbye to our grandparents. Through the window of the compartment we watched as they disembarked from the train and followed an Israeli agent onto a waiting bus. The bus was bound for the airport, where an El Al plane was waiting. We were bound for somewhere else. Where exactly we didn't know—Australia, America, Canada—but someplace that was not Israel. As my mother, aunt, cousin, and I wept, my father and uncle kept an eye out for Israeli agents. These agents were known to inspect compartments. Any indication that we had close relatives on the buses would bring questions: Why were we separating the family? Why were we rejecting our Israeli visas? Why were we so ungrateful to the State of Israel, which had, after all, provided us with the means to escape the Soviet Union?

The answer to these questions, for my father and uncle, was 150 million angry Arabs.

For my grandfather, a lifelong Zionist, this was no answer. Back in Riga, packing our bags, he had decided that he would not go chasing us around the globe. At least in Israel he knew there would be a roof over his head. And at least in Israel, surrounded by 150 million angry Arabs, he would have no trouble identifying the enemy.

In the days leading up to our departure, a common argument went:

Grandfather: There, I'll never have to hear dirty Jew.

Father/Uncle: So instead you'll hear dirty Russian.

Grandfather: Maybe. But where you're going you'll hear one and the other.

Though I never heard dirty Jew, dirty Russian tended to come up. Particularly at Hebrew school. Not very often, but often enough that I felt justified in using it as an excuse when I tried to convince my parents to let me transfer to a normal public school.

This was a campaign I started in earnest in the seventh grade. The year before, we had finally moved out of the apartment building and into a semidetached house. Geographically, the move was negligible—looking out my bedroom window, I could still see our old building—but we now had a backyard, a driveway, a garage for my bicycle, and a carpeted basement. We also now had a neighborhood. Across the street, my aunt and uncle bought a similar house. In other houses lived other Russians who had succeeded in accumulating down payments. Their children became my friends: Eugene, Boris, Alex, Big Vadim, Little Vadim. In the evenings and on the weekends, we roved the streets, played wall ball, road hockey, shoplifted from the Korean's convenience store, and abused Fat Larissa, the neighborhood slut.

My new friends were all Jewish, but after my mother framed my bar mitzvah portrait—in which I wore a white tuxedo—they took me outside, held me down, and pummeled my shoulders until my arms went numb.

My mother was categorically against me leaving Hebrew school. This was partly out of deference to my grandfather, but also because of a deep personal conviction. There were reasons why we had left the Soviet Union. She believed that in Canada I should get what I could never have gotten in Latvia. As far as she was concerned, I wasn't leaving Hebrew school until I learned what it was to be a Jew.

My father, I knew, was more sympathetic. For years, because of special considerations made for the poor Russian Jews, the Hebrew school had subsidized my tuition, but after we bought the house, the subsidy was revoked. And even though my mother had secured a better job and my father's business had improved, I saw the irritation on his face every time I started complaining about the school.

—He knows the language. He can read all the prayers. If he wants to leave maybe we should let him leave already?

—Take the money from my salary.

—I didn't say it was the money.

—Take the money from my salary.

—You want to redo the kitchen. That's also from your salary.

—If that's my choice, I can live without the kitchen.

My mother was resolute. Nothing I said helped my case. So that April, just after Passover, I put Jerry Ackerman in the hospital.

Most days, on his way to the office, my father would drop me off at school in his red 1970 Volvo. On a Friday, after gym, Jerry Ackerman said something about Solly Birnbaum's small hairless penis and Solly started to cry. Solly was fat, had webbed toes, and was reduced to tears at the end of every gym class. I had never defended him before but I seized my chance.

—Ackerman, if I had your tweezer-dick I wouldn't talk.

—Why are you looking at my dick, faggot?

—Ackerman thought he had a pubic hair until he pissed out of it.

—Fuck you, Berman, and that red shitbox your father drives.

In Rabbi Gurvich's office, Dr. Ackerman said that I had banged Jerry's head so hard against the wall that I had given him a concussion. Dr. Ackerman said that Jerry had vomited three times that night and that they'd had to drive him to the hospital at two in the morning. Dr. Ackerman asked, what kind of sick person, what kind of animal would do this? When I refused to answer, my mother apologized to Dr. and Mrs. Ackerman and also to Jerry.

This wasn't the first time my mother and I had been called into Gurvich's office. After our move into the new neighborhood I had begun to affect a hoodlum persona. At school, I kept to myself, glowered in the hallways, and, with the right kind of provocation, punched people in the face. Less than a month before I gave Jerry Ackerman his concussion, I'd gotten into a fight with two eighth graders. Because of dietary laws, the school prohibited bringing meat for lunch. Other students brought peanut butter or tuna fish, but I—and most of the other Russians—would invariably arrive at school with smoked Hungarian salami, Polish bologna, roast turkey. Our mothers couldn't comprehend why anyone would choose to eat peanuts in a country that didn't know what it meant to have a shortage of smoked meat. And so, I was already sensitive about my lunch when the two eighth graders stopped by my table and asked me how I liked my pork sandwich.

For my fight with Jerry Ackerman, I received a two-day suspension. Sparing words, Gurvich made it clear that this was never to happen again. The next time he saw me in his office would be the last. To hit someone's head against a wall—

did I ever think what that could do? If I got so much as within ten feet of Ackerman he didn't want to say what would happen. He asked me if I understood. My mother said I understood. He asked me if I had anything to say. I knew that what I had to say was not what he wanted to hear.

On the drive home my mother asked me what I was trying to do, and when my father got home he came as close as he ever had to hitting me.

—Don't think you're so smart. What do you think happens if you get expelled? You want to repeat the grade? We already paid for the entire year.

On the street, I told Boris, Alex, and Eugene, but they weren't impressed.

—Congratulations, you're the toughest kid in Hebrew school.

I returned to school the week of Holocaust Remembrance Day—which we called Holocaust Day for short. It was one of a series of occasions that punctuated the school year beginning with Rosh Hashanah in September and ending with Israeli Independence Day in May. For Chanukah, the school provided jelly donuts and art class was spent making swords and shields out of papier-mâché; for Purim, everyone dressed up in costume and a pageant was organized during which we all cheered the hanging of evil Hamman and his ten evil sons; for Passover, every class held a preparatory seder and took a field trip to the matzoh bakery; for Israeli Independence Day, we dressed in blue and white and marched around the school yard waving flags and singing the *Hatikvah*, our national anthem.

Holocaust Day was different. Preparations were made days

in advance. The long basement hallway, from the gymnasium to the pool, was converted into a Holocaust museum. Out of storage came the pictures pasted on bristol board. There were photocopies of Jewish passports, there were archival photos of Jews in cattle cars, starving Jews in ghettos, naked Ukrainian Jews waiting at the edge of an open trench, Jews with their hands on barbed wire waiting to be liberated, ovens, schematic drawings of the gas chambers, pictures of empty cans of Zyklon B. Other bristol boards had Yiddish songs written in the ghettos, in the camps. We had crayon drawings done by children in Theresienstadt. We had a big map of Europe with multicolored pins and accurate statistics. Someone's grandfather donated his striped Auschwitz pajamas, someone else's grandmother contributed a jacket with a yellow star on it. There were also sculptures. A woman kneeling with a baby in her arms in bronze. A tin reproduction of the gates of Birkenau with the words *Arbeit Macht Frei*. Sculptures of flaming Stars of David, sculptures of piles of shoes, sculptures of sad bearded Polish rabbis. In the center of the hallway was a large menorah, and all along the walls were smaller memorial candles—one candle for each European country. On Holocaust Day, the fluorescents were extinguished and we moved through the basement by dim candlelight.

Holocaust Day was also the one day that Rabbi Gurvich supervised personally. Gurvich's father was a Holocaust survivor and had, that year, published his memoirs. We were all encouraged to buy the book. When the copies arrived, Gurvich led his father from class to class so that the old man could sign them. Whereas Gurvich was imposing—dark, unsmiling, possessing a gruff seismic voice—his father was frail and mild. In our class, the old man perched himself behind the teacher's desk and smiled benignly as he inked each copy with the double imperative: *Yizkor; al tishkach!* Remember; don't forget!

Even though I had spent the two days of my suspension fantasizing about killing Gurvich and Ackerman, I returned to school and avoided them both. Gurvich was easy to avoid. With the exception of Holocaust Day, his primary role was that of disciplinarian and—unless you were called into his office—he was rarely seen. Ackerman was different. The only class we shared was gym, but in the mornings I saw him grinning as I got my books from my locker; at lunch I sat across the cafeteria as he conspired against me; and at recess, if he was playing, then I abstained from tennis-ball soccer.

For Holocaust Day we were called down into the basement by grades. The hallway was long and, arranged in orderly columns, an entire grade could fit into the basement at one time. After Gurvich made the announcement over the intercom, we followed our teachers down. We were quiet on the way and silent once we got there. Some people started crying before we entered the basement; others started to cry when we reached the dimness and saw the photos on the walls. As we filed in, Gurvich stood waiting for us beside the menorah. When everyone was in the basement, the double doors were closed behind us and we waited for Gurvich to begin. Because the hallway was extremely reverberant, Gurvich's deliberate pause was filled with the echo of stifled sobs, and because there were no windows and the pool was so close, the basement was stuffy and reeked of chlorine.

Gurvich began the service by telling us about the six million, about the vicious Nazis, about our history of oppression.

His heavy voice occupied the entire space, and when he intoned the *El Maleh Rachamim*, I felt his voice reach into me, down into that place where my mother said I was supposed to have the thing called my "Jewish soul." Gurvich sang: O God, full of compassion, who dwells on high, grant true rest upon the wings of the Divine Presence. And when he sang this, his harsh baritone filled with grief so that his voice seemed no longer his own; his voice belonged to the six million. Every syllable that came out of his mouth was important. The sounds he made were dictated by centuries of ancestral mourning. I couldn't understand how it was possible for Gurvich not to cry when his voice sounded the way it did.

After Gurvich finished the prayer, we slowly made our way through the memorial. I stopped by photos of the Warsaw ghetto during the uprising and then beside a portrait of Mordecai Anilewicz, the leader of the ghetto resistance. I noticed Ackerman behind me. He was with two friends and I turned my head to look.

—What are you looking at, assface?

I turned away. I concentrated on moving down the hallway but felt a shove from behind and lost my balance. I managed to catch myself along the wall. My hand landed safely on top of a child's crayon drawing, but my foot accidentally knocked over the Czech memorial candle. Everybody in the hallway froze at the sound of the breaking glass. I turned around and saw Ackerman snickering. Matthew Wise, Ackerman's friend, stood between me and Ackerman. Wise was bigger than Ackerman, and I was sure he was the one who had pushed me. Instinctively, I lunged at Wise and tackled him to the ground. I was on top and choking him when Gurvich grabbed the back of my shirt and tried to pull me off. Even as Gurvich pulled me away I held on to Wise's throat. And when Gurvich finally yanked me clear, I saw that Wise was still on the floor, trembling.

While the rest of my class finished going through the memorial, I waited upstairs in Gurvich's office. I waited, also, until the sixth grade went down to the memorial, before Gurvich returned.

I sat for half an hour, maybe longer. I imagined the horrible consequences. I foresaw my mother's reaction and, even worse, my father's reaction. I didn't regret what I had done, but the fear of squandering so much of my parents' money made me physically sick.

When Gurvich finally walked into his office, he didn't sit down. Without looking at me, he told me to get up out of my goddamn chair and go back downstairs. I was not to touch anything, I was not to move, I was to stay there until he came.

Back in the basement I waited for Gurvich by the menorah. I didn't know where else to stand. I didn't know where in the memorial my presence would be the least offensive to Gurvich. I stood in one place beside a picture of Jews looking out of their bunks, and somehow I felt that my standing there would anger Gurvich. I moved over to the sculptures and felt the same way. I wanted to strike some sort of anodyne pose, to make myself look like someone who didn't deserve to be expelled.

I was tracing the ironwork on the menorah when Gurvich pushed the double doors open and entered. Very deliberately, as if he didn't know what to say first, Gurvich walked over to where I stood. I took my hands off the menorah.

—How is it that all of this doesn't mean anything to you, Berman? Can you tell me that?

—It means something.

—It means something? It means something when you

jump on another Jew in this place, on Holocaust Day? This is how you demonstrate it means something?

He raised his voice.

—It means something when you act like an animal to the memory of everyone who died?

—What about Wise? He pushed me into the wall.

—Wise had to go home because of what you did, so don't ask me about Wise. Wise wasn't the one choking another Jew at a memorial for the Holocaust.

I didn't say anything. Gurvich tugged at his beard.

—Look around this, Berman, what do you see?

I looked.

—The Holocaust.

—And does this make you feel anything?

—Yes.

—Yes? It does?

—Yes.

—I don't believe you. I don't believe you feel anything.

He put his hand on my shoulder. He leaned in closer.

—Berman, a Nazi wouldn't do here what you did today. Don't tell me about how you feel.

—I'm not a Nazi.

—No, you're not a Nazi? What are you?

—A Jew.

—What?

—A Jew.

—I can't hear you.

—I'm a Jew.

—Why so quiet, Berman? It's just us here. Don't be so ashamed to say it.

—I'm a Jew, I said into my shoes.

He turned me around by my shoulder. I may have considered myself a tough little bastard, but when Gurvich gripped me I understood that mine was a boy's shoulder and that his was a man's hand. He put his face very close to mine and made me look at him. I could smell the musky staleness of his beard. For the first time, I felt I was going to cry.

—So that my uncles hear you in Treblinka! he commanded.

He tightened his grip on my shoulder until he saw it hurt. I was convinced he was going to hit me. The last thing I wanted to do was start crying, so I started crying.

—I'm a Jew! I shouted into his face.

My voice rang off the walls, and off the sculptures and the pictures and the candles. I had screamed it in his face wishing to kill him, but he only nodded his head. He kept his hand on my shoulder and waited until I really started to sob. My shoulder shuddered under his hand and I heard the repulsive sound of my own whimpering. Finally, Gurvich removed his hand and backed away a half step. As soon as he did, I wanted him to put his hand back. I was standing in the middle of the hallway, shaking. I wanted to sit down on the floor, or lean against a wall, something. Anything but stand in the middle of that hallway while Gurvich nodded his rabbinical head at me. When he was done nodding, he turned away and opened the double doors leading up to the stairs. Halfway out, before closing the doors, Gurvich looked back to where I hadn't moved.

—Now, Berman, he said, now maybe you understand what it is to be a Jew.

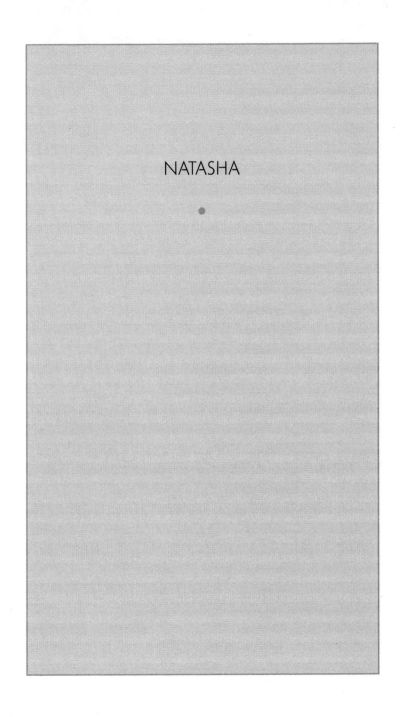

NATASHA

It is the opposite which is good to us.

—HERACLITUS

WHEN I WAS SIXTEEN I was high most of the time. That year my parents bought a new house at the edge of Toronto's sprawl. A few miles north were cows; south the city. I spent most of my time in basements. The suburbs offered nothing and so I lived a subterranean life. At home, separated from my parents by door and stairs, I smoked hash, watched television, read, and masturbated. In other basements I smoked, watched television, and refined my style with girls.

In the spring, my uncle Fima, my grandmother's youngest brother, married his second wife. She arrived from Moscow for two weeks to get acquainted with him and the rest of the family. Dusa, our dentist, had known the woman in Russia and recommended her. She was almost forty and my uncle was forty-four. The woman was the latest in a string of last chances. A previous last chance had led to his first marriage. That marriage, to a fellow Russian immigrant, had failed within six months. My uncle was a good man, a hard worker, and a polymath. He read books, newspapers, and travel brochures. He could speak with equal authority about the Crimean War and the Toronto Maple Leafs. Short months after arriving in Toronto he took a job giving tours of the city to visiting Russians. But he wasn't rich and never would be.

He was also honest to a fault and nervous with people. My grandmother's greatest fear was that he would always be alone in the world.

Zina, the woman, had greasy brown hair cut in a mannish style. She was thin, her body almost without contour. The first time I saw her was when my uncle brought her to our house for dinner. She wore tight blue pants, high heels, and a yellow silk blouse which accentuated her conspicuously long nipples. The top buttons of her blouse were undone and a thin gold chain with a Star of David clung to her breastbone. When she kissed me in greeting she smelled of sweat and lilac.

Zina strode into our house as if she were on familiar territory, and her confidence had the effect of making my uncle act as though he were the stranger. He stumbled through the introductions and almost knocked over his chair. He faltered as he tried to explain how they had spent the day and Zina chided him and finished his sentences. When my mother served the raspberry torte, Zina fed my uncle from her fork. In Russia she was a "teacher of English" and she sprinkled her conversation with English words and phrases. The soup my mother served was "tasty," our dining room "divine," and my father "charming." After dinner, in the living room, she placed her hand on my uncle's knee. I was, as usual, high, and I became fixated on the hand. It rested on my uncle's knee like a small pale animal. Sometimes it would arch or rise completely to make a point, always to settle back on the knee. Under her hand, my uncle's knee barely moved.

After her two weeks in Canada, Zina returned to Moscow. Before she left, my mother and aunt took her shopping and bought her a new wardrobe. They believed that Zina would be good for my uncle. The last thing he needed was a timid wife. Maybe she was a little aggressive, but to make it in this country you couldn't apologize at every step like him. My grand-mother was anxious because Zina had a young daughter in Moscow, but she conceded that at this age to find a woman without a child probably meant there was something wrong with her. My uncle did not disagree. There were positives and negatives, he said.

The decision was made quickly and days after Zina's departure my uncle wrote her a letter inviting her to return and become his wife. One month later, Zina was back in Toronto. This time, my entire family went to the airport to greet her. We stood at the gate and waited as a stream of Russian faces filtered by. Near the end of the stream, Zina appeared. She was wearing an outfit my mother had purchased for her. She carried a heavy suitcase. When she saw my uncle she dropped the suitcase and ran to him and kissed him on his cheeks and on his mouth. A thin blond girl, also carrying a suitcase, picked up Zina's abandoned bag and dragged both suitcases through the gate. The girl had large blue eyes and her straight blond hair was cut into bangs. She strained toward us with the bags and stopped behind Zina. She waited patiently, her face without expression, for her mother to introduce her. Her name was Natasha. She was fourteen. My mother said, Meet your new cousin. Later, as we drove my grandparents home, my grandmother despaired that the girl's father was obviously a shaygets.

One week after their arrival, everyone went down to North York City Hall for the civil ceremony. A retired judge administered the vows and we took photos in the atrium. There was no rabbi, no chuppah, no stomping of the glass. Afterward, we all went to our house for a barbecue. One after another people made toasts. My uncle and Zina sat at the head of the table like a real married couple. For a wedding gift they were given money to help them rent a larger apartment. My uncle's one-bedroom would not do. This wasn't Russia and the girl couldn't continue to sleep in the living room. The one time my grandparents had gone to visit, Natasha emerged from the shower naked and, without so much as acknowledging their presence, went into the kitchen for an apple. While my grandparents tried to listen to my uncle and Zina talk about Zina's plans to get her teaching certificate, Natasha stood in the kitchen and ate the apple.

At the barbecue, my mother seated Natasha between me and my cousin, Jana. It was our duty to make her feel welcome. She was new to the country, she had no friends, she spoke no English, she was now family. Jana, almost two years my senior, had no interest in a fourteen-year-old girl. Especially one who dressed like a Polish hooker, didn't speak English, and wasn't saying anything in Russian either. Midway through the barbecue, a car full of girls came for Jana and Natasha became my responsibility. My mother encouraged me to show her around the house.

Without enthusiasm I led Natasha around the house. Without enthusiasm she followed. For lack of anything else to say, I would enter a room and announce its name in Russian. We entered the kitchen and I said kitchen, my parents' bedroom and I said bedroom, the living room, which I called the room where we watch television since I had no idea what it was called in Russian. Then I walked her down into the basement. Through the blinds we could see the backyard and the legs of our newly incarnated family. I said, That's it, the whole house. Natasha looked around the room and then shut the blinds, rendering the already dim basement almost dark. She dropped down into one of the two velour beanbag chairs I had in front of the television. Chairs that I had been earnestly and consistently humping since the age of twelve.

—You have all of this to yourself?

—Yes.

—It must be nice.

—It is.

—What do you do here?

—Watch television, read.

—That's it?

—That's most of it.

—Do you bring girls here?

—Not really.

—Have you had sex down here?

—What?

—You don't have to say if you don't want to. I don't really care. It doesn't mean anything.

—You're fourteen.

—So what? That doesn't mean anything either. I've done it a hundred times. If you want, I'll do it with you.

—We're cousins.

—No we're not.

—Your mother married my uncle.

—It's too bad. He's nice.

—He is.

—I feel sorry for him. She'll ruin his life.

—It's hard to imagine his life getting worse.

—She'll make it worse.

—She's your mother.

—She's a whore. Do you want to know how it sounds when they do it?

—Not particularly.

—They do it at least three times a day. He groans like he is being killed and she screams like she is killing him.

A month after the wedding, my uncle, Zina, and Natasha rented a new two-bedroom apartment ten minutes' walk from our house. This was in the early summer and I was on vacation from school. Instead of going off to camp I made an arrangement to work for Rufus, my dealer. Over the course of the year we had become friends. He was twenty and, while keeping up his business, was also studying philosophy at the University of Toronto. Aside from providing me with drugs, he also recommended books. Because of him I graduated from John Irving and Mordecai Richler to Camus, Heraclitus, Catullus, and Kafka. That summer, in exchange for doing the deliveries, I got free dope—plus whatever I shorted off potheads—and a little money. I also got to borrow the books Rufus had been reading over the course of the year. This, to me, was a perfectly legitimate way to spend two months, although my parents insisted that I had to find a job. Telling them about the job I already had was out of the question, and so the summer started off on a point of conflict.

A week into my summer vacation, my mother resolved our conflict. If I had no intention of finding a job, she would put me to good use. Since I was home by myself I would be conscripted into performing an essential service. I was alone and Natasha was alone. She didn't know anyone in the city and was making a nuisance of herself. From what I could understand, she wasn't actually doing anything to be a nuisance, but her mere presence in the apartment was inconvenient. My family felt that my uncle needed time alone with his new wife and having Natasha around made him uncomfortable. Besides, she was difficult. My uncle reported that she refused to speak to her mother and literally hadn't said a word in weeks.

The morning after my mother decided that I would keep Natasha company I was on my way to my uncle's new apartment. I hadn't seen him, Zina, or Natasha since the wedding and the barbecue. They hadn't been back to our house and I had had no reason to go there. In fact, in all the years that my uncle lived in Toronto I had never been to his apartment. Despite occasional invitations, I avoided the place because I preferred not to see how he lived.

By the time I arrived, my uncle had already left for work. Zina met me at the door wearing a blue Soviet housedress that could have passed for a hospital gown. Again, she wore no bra. I was greeted by nipples, then Zina. She put her hand on my arm and ushered me into the kitchen, where she was filling out forms to obtain credentials from the school board. A stack of forms was laid out on the table along with black bread and cucumbers. She made me a sandwich I did not want and told me what a wonderful man my uncle was. How she was very fortunate to find such a man and how good things would be as soon as Natasha became accustomed to their new life. We were co-conspirators, she and I, both working for Natasha's well-being. She was convinced that I would be able to help her. She sensed that Natasha liked me. Natasha didn't like many people.

—I'm her mother, and no matter what she says, I would cut off my right arm for her. But she has always been different. Even as a baby she hardly smiled.

Zina led me to Natasha's door and knocked. Through the door she announced that I was here. After a brief pause Natasha opened the door. She was wearing blue jeans and a souvenir T-shirt from Niagara Falls. I could see behind her into the room. There was a small bed and a table. On one wall was an old poster of Michael Jackson circa *Thriller*. In bold red letters a phonetic approximation of Michael Jackson's name was written in Cyrillic. I read the name slowly letter by letter since I was effectively illiterate. It gave me something to do while Natasha and Zina glared at each other in acrimonious silence.

—I'm an enemy because I took her away from her criminal friends. I'm an enemy because I wanted to give her a better life. Now she won't say a word, but one day she'll thank me.

Without breaking her silence, Natasha grabbed my hand and led me out of the apartment. As we went past the door Zina called after us telling me to watch out for Natasha. I was to make sure that she didn't do anything stupid. Natasha should remember what it would do to my uncle if something were to happen to her. Even if she didn't care about how Zina felt, she should at least consider my uncle, for whom she was now like a daughter.

In the stairway Natasha released my hand and we descended to the back of the building and the parking lot. Outside, she turned and spoke what must have been her first words in weeks.

—I can't stand looking at her. I want to scratch out my eyes. In Moscow I never had to see her. Now she's always there.

We wound our way out of the parking lot and toward the subdivisions leading back to my house. On the way I decided to stop at Rufus's and pick up an eighth for one of our regular heads. Rufus had a house not far from us, and since it was still early in the morning I knew that he would be home. I walked ahead and Natasha trailed along, more interested in the uniform lawns and houses than the specifics of where we were going. Aside from the odd Filipina nanny wheeling a little white kid, the streets were quiet. The sun was neither bright nor hot and the outdoors felt conveniently like the indoors: God's thermostat set to "suburban basement."

—In Moscow, everyone lives in apartments. The only time you see houses like this is in the country, where people have their dachas.

—Three years ago this was the country.

We found Rufus on his backyard deck listening to Led Zeppelin, eating an omelette. Although he was alone the table was set for four with a complete set of linen napkins and matching cutlery. Rufus didn't seem at all surprised to see us. That was part of his persona. Rufus never appeared surprised about anything. At twenty years old he had already accomplished more than most men twice his age. It was rumored that aside from dealing Rufus was also a partner in a used car lot/body shop and various other ventures. Nobody who knew him had ever seen him sleep.

Even though I had only intended to see Rufus for as long as it took to get the eighth, he insisted on cooking us breakfast. Natasha and I sat at the kitchen counter as Rufus made more omelettes. He explained that even when he ate alone he liked to set a full table. The mere act of setting extra places prevented him from receding into solipsism. It also made for good karma, so that even when he was not expecting guests there existed tangible evidence announcing that he was open to the possibility.

While Rufus spoke Natasha's eyes roamed around the house, taking in the spotless kitchen, the copper cookware, the living room with matching leather sofas, the abstract art on the walls. If not for the contents of the basement refrigerator, the house gave no indication that it was owned and inhabited by a drug dealer barely out of his teens. This was no accident. Rufus believed that it helped his business. His clients were all middle-class suburban kids, and despite his bohemian inclinations, a nice house in the suburbs was the perfect loca- tion. It kept him local and it meant that, for his customers, a visit to their dealer felt just like coming home.

Back on the deck I explained to Rufus about Natasha, leaving out certain details I didn't think he needed to know. As Rufus and I talked, Natasha sat contentedly with her omelette and orange juice. Since we'd left my uncle's apart- ment her attitude toward everything had taken a form of benign detachment. She was calibrated somewhere between resignation and joy.

I noticed Rufus looking at her.

—Did I mention she was fourteen?

—My interest, I assure you, is purely anthropological.

—The anthropology of jailbait.

—She's an intense little chick.

—She's Russian. We're born intense.

—With all due respect, Berman, you and her aren't even the same species.

To get her attention Rufus leaned across the table and tapped Natasha on the arm. She looked up from her omelette and re- turned Rufus's smile. He asked me to translate for him. His own family, he said, could be traced back to Russia. He wanted to know what Russia was like now. What it was really like.

With a shrug Natasha answered.

—Russia is shit but people enjoy themselves.

After that first day, Natasha started coming to our house regu- larly. I no longer went to pick her up but waited instead for her to arrive. Through my basement window I could see her as she appeared in our backyard and wandered around inspecting my mother's peonies or the raspberry and red currant bushes. If I was in a certain mood I would watch her for a while before going upstairs and opening the sliding glass door in the kitchen. Other times, I would just go and open the door. We spent most of our days in the basement. I read and Natasha studied television English. When I had a delivery to make she accompanied me. Between reading, television English, and deliveries, I taught Natasha how to get high. I showed her how to roll a joint, to light a pipe, or, in a pinch, where to cut the holes in a Coke can or Gatorade bottle. In exchange, Natasha taught me other things. Many of these things had nothing to do with sex.

After our days in the basement we would listen for my mother to arrive home from work. To avoid some serious unpleasantness I made a habit of setting my alarm for five o'clock. If we weren't sleeping, the alarm simply reminded us to open a window or get dressed. By the time my mother came home we were usually in the kitchen or out in the backyard. Chores that had been assigned to me were usually done at this time. It pleased my mother to come home and find me, spade in hand, turning over the earth around the berry bushes. Also, once it was established that Natasha much preferred to stay at our house, my mother grew more than accustomed to having her around. Unlike me and my father, Natasha volunteered to help her in the kitchen. The two of them would stand at the sink peeling potatoes and slicing up radishes and cucumbers for salad. I often came in to overhear my mother telling stories about her childhood in postwar Latvia—a land of outhouses, horse-drawn wagons, and friendly neighbors. In Natasha she found a receptive audience.

They spoke the same language—Russian girl to Russian girl. This despite the fact that, in too many ways, Natasha's childhood couldn't have been more different from my mother's if she had been raised by Peruvian cannibals, but there was never any indication of this in our kitchen. Only my mother telling stories and Natasha listening.

Very quickly, our family of three became a family of four. No more than two weeks after I picked her up at my uncle's apartment Natasha became a fixture at our house. It was a situation that, for different and even perversely conflicting reasons, suited everyone. It solved the Natasha problem for my uncle. It solved the Zina problem for Natasha. It made my mother feel like she was protecting my uncle's last chance at happiness and also satisfying her own latent desire for a daughter. It absolved me of the need to find a job and cast me in a generally favorable light with the rest of my family. And, strangely enough, Natasha's incorporation into the household made the things we did in the basement seem less bad. Or not bad at all. What we did in the basement became only a part of who we were. There were layers upon layers. Which was why, at any one moment, I felt for Natasha the most natural and unusual feelings; to explain the feelings would be impossible, but whatever they were they were never bad.

Since I had been conditioned to approach sex as negotiation, I was amazed to discover that it could be as perfunctory as brushing your teeth. One day, after some but not too many days together, Natasha simply slid out of her jeans and removed her shirt. We were sitting inches apart, each on our own beanbag. Moments before, we had finished smoking a joint and I had gone back to Kafka's diaries. I became aware of what she was doing slower than a sixteen-year-old should have. I looked over as she was wriggling out of her pants. That she saw me looking changed nothing. On the beanbag, naked, she turned to me and said, very simply, as if it were as insignificant to her as it was significant to me: Do you want to? At sixteen, no expert but no virgin, I lived in a permanent state of want to. But for everything I knew, I knew almost nothing. In the middle of the day, Natasha in the basement, was the first time I had seen a live naked girl. All the parts available for viewing. Nothing in my previous dimly lit gropings compared. In my teenage life, what was more elusive than a properly illuminated naked girl? And the fact that it was Natasha—my nominal cousin, fourteen, strange—no longer mattered. After spending days with her and thinking about her at night, I knew very well how I felt. And so, when she asked if I wanted to, I wanted to.

That day was the first of many firsts. With the house to ourselves and no threat of being disturbed, we did everything I had ever dreamed of doing—including some things that hadn't even occurred to me. We showered together, we slept in the same bed, I watched her walk across the room, I watched her pee. These prosaic things, being new, were as exciting as the sex. And for me the sex was as much about the variation as the pleasure. Much of the pleasure was in the variation. I kept a mental list from position to position, crossing off one accomplishment after another. Nothing was repeated until everything was attempted. That way, in the event that I was struck by a bus, I would feel as though I had lived a full life. Most of the things we did Natasha had already done, but she was perfectly happy to oblige. If she was doing it as a favor, she never expected gratitude and demanded nothing in return.

In our quieter moments Natasha told me about the men who had taken her picture. She had never minded any of it, but she never understood why they couldn't explain why they liked one thing over another. They had always known exactly how they wanted her to look but none of them could give her a reason. Why did they prefer her leg raised this way and not that, why squatting from behind or holding her hand in a certain position? Some of the positions had been practically identical, and yet they had insisted on them. The only explanation they offered was that it looked good, or that it was sexy. And yet she never felt that way about men. She never cared how they looked, or what side she was viewing them from.

—You don't care how I look?

—You look how you look. If you bent over it wouldn't make any difference to me.

I bent over.

—That doesn't make any difference?

—It looks stupid. But what if I bend over? Does it look stupid?

—No, it looks good.

—Why is that?

—It just does.

—You can't explain it?

I thought it had to do with the forbidden. The attraction to the forbidden in the forbidden. The forbiddenest. But it still wasn't much of an answer.

At the same time that things with Natasha were improving my mother started to hear the first rumblings of trouble in my uncle's marriage. My grandparents, who had been accustomed to visiting my uncle frequently, were informed that maybe they shouldn't come over quite so often. Their habit of arriving unannounced was aggravating Zina, who insisted that she had too much to worry about without always having to accommodate my grandparents. My grandmother, although hurt, naturally made excuses for both my uncle and Zina. We were a close family, she said, but not all people can be expected to be the same way. Also, with time, as Zina became more comfortable, she was certain that she would feel differently. In any case, as long as my uncle was happy she was prepared to respect Zina's wishes. My uncle, for his part, said nothing. The signals were mixed. There was what my grandmother said, but my mother also knew that he and Zina took a weekend trip together to Niagara-on-the-Lake and another to Quebec City. After Quebec City my uncle sported a new leather jacket and a gray Stetson. Whatever was happening between them, he wasn't complaining.

I heard all of these things through my mother, but I also heard other things from Natasha. I now knew more about my uncle's life than I ever had, and certainly more than anyone else in my family. I knew, for instance, that he now spent as many nights on the living room couch as he did in the bedroom. I knew that Zina was racking up long-distance bills to Moscow, calling Natasha's father, a drunk who had effectively abandoned them years ago. She called in the mornings as soon as my uncle left for work and made various and emphatic promises. Natasha had seen her father only infrequently as a child, and was perfectly content to go the rest of her life without seeing him again. She could say the same thing about her mother. Essentially, since the age of eight, she had been on her own. Going to school, coming home, cooking her own dinners, running around with friends. Zina, when not at work, was chasing after Natasha's father or bringing random men into the apartment. As much as possible, Natasha avoided her.

When Natasha was twelve a friend of hers told her about a man who paid ten dollars for some pictures of her. The girl had gone and taken a shower in the man's bathroom and he had not only paid her but also bought her dinner. He had promised her the same again if she could bring a friend. Ten dollars each for taking a shower. Natasha remembered thinking that the man had to be an idiot. She went, took her shower, and collected her ten dollars. There wasn't much to it and it wasn't as boring as hanging out at her friend's apartment. And ten dollars was ten dollars. Zina hardly gave her anything, and so it was good to have some of her own money.

After that man was another who took pictures of her and some friends in the forest. He had them climb birch trees and lie down in a meadow. He asked some of the girls to hold hands and kiss each other. Another man took some photos of her in her school uniform. None of these men touched her, but she wouldn't have cared if they had. They were nice and she felt sorry for them.

All of this led eventually to a Soviet director who had gone from working at the Moscow studios to making pornographic movies for Western businessmen. The man had a dacha on the outskirts of the city and would send a car around to pick up Natasha and her friends. Some of these friends were girls, some boys. They would spend the day at the dacha eating, drinking, having a good time. At some point the director would shoot some movies of them. Aside from teenagers there were also older women. On the first day, Natasha watched the women have sex. She understood that doing it or not doing it was not a serious consideration. In the end, everyone did it. If not in movies, then somewhere else, and it made absolutely no difference one way or the other. The only thing about having sex at the dacha was that it was much more pleasant. The house was beautiful and there was a large lawn and a forest. There was also a *banya* and a Jacuzzi. The filming itself didn't even take very long. The rest of the time they just relaxed. She was never asked to do anything she didn't want to, and she never saw anyone else do something that she wouldn't have done herself. Even though she and her friends knew they wouldn't be at the dacha if it weren't for the movies, the sex never felt as though it were the focus. The director and the other men became their friends. They treated them very well. And if they wanted to sleep with the girls, the girls could see no reason why not. At the end of the day everyone got twenty-five dollars.

Natasha didn't have any of the pictures or movies, which was disappointing since I wanted to see them. But it wasn't like she was a model. She didn't keep an album of pictures to show to prospective photographers. She was the album. They looked at her and preferred not to know about her past. And without having pictures around there was no risk of Zina finding out what Natasha was doing. Not that she thought Zina would care, instead it was that Natasha suspected Zina would want the money. In any case, when Zina did finally find out it was only because she heard something from another girl's mother. And much as Natasha expected, Zina told her that if she was going to be a whore she could at least help out with the rent. Natasha never felt like a whore. She didn't do it for the money, but she also wasn't so stupid as to turn it down. If anyone was a whore, it was Zina. And she came cheap. She sold herself to Natasha's father for nothing, and the men she brought to the apartment treated her like filth. They paid her with curses and bruises.

I carried all this information around like a prize. It was my connection to a larger darker world. At Rufus's parties it allowed me to feel superior to the other stoner acolytes comparing Nietzsche to Bob Marley. I took Natasha to these parties and she stood quietly listening to our incoherent and impassioned conversations. Later she would surprise me with just how much she had understood. By midsummer, if called upon, Natasha could answer basic questions and had learned enough to know when to tell someone to fuck off. The other stoners liked more than anything to hear Natasha say fuck off in her crisp Moscow accent. In crude canine fashion, they accepted Natasha as one of their own. Natasha was cool.

We coasted this way into August when Zina appeared in our backyard one evening during dinner. The way she looked, it was clear that something horrible was about to happen. My mother opened the sliding door and Zina burst into our kitchen and inaccurately described what Natasha and I had been doing. Then screams, sobbing, and hysterics. I watched as my father wrenched Natasha from her mother, her teeth leaving a bloody wound on Zina's hand. Zina let fly a torrent of invective, most of which I couldn't understand. But I understood enough to know that what was happening in the kitchen was nothing compared with what was to come. Zina threatened to call the police, to place an ad in the Russian newspaper, to personally knock on all of our neighbors' doors. Natasha thrashed in my father's grip and freed herself enough to lunge unsuccessfully for a bread knife. She shrieked that her mother was a liar. I sat in my chair, nauseated, contemplating lies and escape.

After my father bandaged Zina's hand she waited outside while my mother talked with Natasha and me. With Zina outside my mother fumbled for the proper way to pose the question. It was hard to believe that what Zina was saying was true, but why would she make something like this up. Natasha said that it was because her mother hated her and never wanted her to be happy. She was jealous that Natasha was happy with us and wanted to ruin it, just as she had dragged Natasha from Moscow even though she hadn't wanted to go. Zina hated her and wanted to ruin her life, that was all. When my mother turned to me I denied everything. Unless Zina produced pictures or video I wasn't admitting a thing. I was terrified but I wasn't a moron.

When it became obvious that we had reached an impasse, my mother called my uncle. He came to our house in a state of anxiety that was remarkable even for him. He sat down between my mother and Zina on the living room couch. I was beside my father, who was in his armchair, and Natasha stood rigidly with her back against the door. My uncle confessed that he didn't know what was happening. Everything had been fine. What situation doesn't have problems, but on the whole he was content. The only explanation he could propose was that all of this might have had to do with a fight between Zina and Natasha over a phone bill. There had been a very expensive bill to Russia, almost six hundred dollars, which Zina had said were calls to her mother. He could understand that while getting used to a new life Zina would want to talk to her mother. Also, her mother was alone in Moscow and missed her. It was only natural that there would be calls. That there were so many was unfortunately a financial and not a personal problem. If it was within his means, he would be happy if Zina talked to her mother as much as she liked. But as it was, he had suggested that she try to be more careful about the amount of time she spent on the phone. They talked about it and she said she understood. It was then that Natasha accused Zina of lying to him and said she wanted her mother to tell him the truth about who she had been calling. This started a fight. But at no point did he hear anything about me and Natasha. He was certain it wasn't true and was just something between a mother and daughter. Everyone was still getting used to things and it would be a mistake to make too much of it. In a day or so everyone would calm down and it would be forgotten.

That night my uncle, Zina, and Natasha slept at our house. Natasha in the guest room, Zina on the downstairs couch, and my uncle on the floor beside her. Zina refused to leave the house without Natasha and Natasha refused to leave with Zina. I was relegated to my basement. In the morning Natasha had indeed calmed down and she agreed to return home with Zina and my uncle. Forgoing breakfast, the three of them walked out the door neither looking at or touching one another. As we watched them go my mother announced that she had now seen enough craziness to last a lifetime. Whatever the truth, she knew one thing for certain: Natasha and I were kaput.

The following day, after hours of waiting, I left the house and headed for Rufus's. Books, bong, television; no distraction could eclipse the greater distraction of Natasha's absence. I was alone in my basement, she was up eleven floors with Zina—I couldn't understand why she didn't come. Our afternoons could still be ours. My mother's proscription didn't have to be obeyed between nine and five. Had the situation been reversed, I would not have disappointed her. Despite everything that had happened the previous night, I couldn't see why anything needed to change. Clearly, judging from the teeth marks on Zina's hand, Natasha wasn't Zina's source of information. And even though Zina's accusation happened to be more true than not, it appeared to be an unfortunate raving coincidence rather than something she could confirm. I didn't see why I had to suffer because of a lunatic.

A pool company's van was parked outside Rufus's and I followed the sound of voices into the backyard. In the middle of the yard, Rufus stood with two men from the pool company. Guys in jeans and golf shirts with the pool company's logo stitched on the breast pocket. The three were talking like old friends, each with a beer in hand, discussing the possible dimensions of a possible pool. Rufus invited me to contribute to the deliberations. If the price was right they could start digging tomorrow.

I had never known Rufus to be much of a swimmer; on nights when some of the other stoners and I would hop the fences of neighborhood pools, he rarely participated.

—Do you even swim?

—Berman, nobody swims in these things. They're for floating. Fill them up with plastic inflatables and free-associate. Gentle swaying stimulates the brainpan.

I watched the pool guys pacing off most of his yard.

—Why not start with a hammock and work your way up?

—Sometimes I'm out here and I need to take a leak. But I don't want to go inside. The weather's nice. I want to stay out but I need to pee. Just for that the pool would be worth the investment.

—You could pee on the bushes.

—I'm a suburban homeowner, there's a social contract. Pissing in the pool is fine but whipping out your dick and irrigating the shrubbery is bad news. It's all about property value.

I settled back on Rufus's deck and waited for the pool guys to leave. I had no deliveries to make that morning and I had neglected to bring along the books I was supposed to return to him. I was there without the veneer of pretext. After escorting the pool guys back to their van Rufus joined me on the deck.

—Where's the girl?

—With her mother.

—I thought she hated her mother.

—She does.

—So what are you doing here? Go liberate her.

—It's forbidden.

—You're sixteen, everything is forbidden. The world expects you to disobey.

—I've been accused of unnatural acts.

—Society was founded on unnatural acts. Read the Bible. You start with Adam and Eve, after that if somebody doesn't boink a sibling it's end of story.

—You mind if I use that argument with my mother?

Rufus got up and looked out across his yard.

—What do you think about a hot tub?

—Instead of the pool?

—With the pool. Do everything in mosaic tile. Give it a real Greek feel. Put up some Doric columns. Get a little fountain. Eat grapes. Play Socrates.

He descended from the deck and walked to the corner of his yard and struck a pose that was either Socrates or the fountain. Our conversation was over.

From Rufus's I walked to my uncle's building and lurked until an old man was buzzed in by another old man. Romeo climbed a trellis, so I took the stairs. Eleven flights later I was in the hallway, passing the smells of other apartments. With one or two exceptions all the doorposts had mezuzahs, just like the hallways above and below. Everyone conveniently assembled for UJA solicitors and neo-Nazis.

I knocked and Zina opened the door. She was wearing the same blue housedress. She blocked the doorway so that it was hard to see beyond her into the apartment. At first she said nothing. I had prepared myself for the worst, but she seemed pleased to see me.

—I wanted to apologize to you myself. I don't blame you for what happened. It wasn't your fault. She has turned grown men inside out and you're just a boy. It was crazy to expect anything else. I know how weak men are. I am to blame. The life in Russia was like a disease to children. Natasha is a very sick girl.

Behind Zina I noticed a movement. It was Natasha. I could see her over Zina's shoulder. She stood at the far end of the apartment, leaning against the living room couch. When I caught her eyes they reflected nothing. They were no less remote than the first time I saw her at the airport. She continued looking in my direction, but I couldn't discern if she was looking at me or the back of Zina's head. Zina, sensing Natasha's presence, turned to look at her daughter. When she looked back at me, her turning was a motion that included the closing of the door.

—It will be best for everybody if you didn't see Natasha anymore.

Late that night, after a day spent missing Natasha, despairing over the black void that was the remainder of my summer and my life in general, Natasha knocked on my basement window. I woke up and cupped my hands against the glass to see out. By the sound of the knock I knew it was her. I looked out and saw her squatting like a Vietnamese peasant in front of the window. In the dark it was hard to see her face. Upstairs in the kitchen I opened the sliding glass door and went into the yard to join her. She was hugging her knees at the base of our pine tree; her suitcase, the same one I had seen at the airport, was lying on the grass beside her. When I got close enough I could see that she had been crying. I joined her on the grass. Already, after only one day apart and remembering the way she had looked at me over Zina's shoulder, I didn't feel as though I could touch her.

—You listened to her lies. Why did you listen to her lies?

—What was I supposed to do?

—You could have knocked her down. You could have broken down the door.

—And what then?

—I don't know. Something. Something else would have happened. But you left me alone with her.

—You looked right at me. Why didn't you say anything?

—But I already told you everything. You saw how she tried to ruin my life and your life and how she was killing your uncle. You knew all of this but you didn't do anything. You're like your uncle. You want people to make decisions for you.

Natasha picked at the grass. Tears welled up in her eyes. She let them fall. I got up and picked up her suitcase. It felt empty and weighed almost nothing. I made a move toward the house.

—What are you doing?

—Taking it inside.

—I can't go inside. I can't stay here. I have to leave.

—You have to leave tonight?

—Do you want to come with me?

—Where?

—Florida. One of the businessmen who came to the dacha

lives there. He is very rich. He promised that if I ever came to Florida he would give me a job. He'll give you one too.

—We have to decide this tonight?

—Yes. I can't stay here and I can't go home. There is no more home. My mother has left your uncle. I can't live with her and I can't stay with him. I have nowhere to go.

—What do you mean your mother left my uncle?

—I forced them to decide.

I put the suitcase back down.

—She made him sleep on the couch again. I went out to the living room. At first he was asleep but when he woke up and understood what was happening he didn't stop me. He knew whose mouth it was. And then she heard and came out of the bedroom. He needed me to do it that way or he would never have gotten away from her. I wasn't going to let her ruin his life. I wasn't going to let her win.

Strangely, my first thought was about my grandmother. My next thought was that my uncle would kill himself.

—He let her insult him, embarrass him, steal his money. But he wouldn't leave her. He was a coward. So I gave him a coward's reason to leave. It's funny, other men would have felt the opposite way. They would have taken it as a reason to stay and spent the next two years fucking me.

I helped Natasha back down into the basement and promised her that I would wake her before my parents got up. I gave her my bed and slept on the floor. When the alarm rang I dug out all the money I had and gave it to her. It amounted to a little more than a hundred dollars. I watched her drag her suitcase down our street, heading in the direction of the bus station and Florida.

When my parents woke up the phones were already ringing. My uncle had arrived on my grandparents' doorstep at seven in the morning. His marriage was over. This confirmed my grandmother's suspicions. From the first she had felt something wasn't right with Zina. That her daughter was the product of a shaygets should have been enough. Now my uncle was without an apartment and he was financially obligated for Zina and Natasha because of the sponsorship papers he had signed. As to why the separation had to be so drastic, why he couldn't stay in the apartment until he found a new place, my uncle was vague. They could no longer live together. Nobody in my family asked about Natasha or even knew that she had left home. As far as the family was concerned, once my uncle severed his relationship with Zina, she and Natasha ceased to exist.

For days afterward I stayed in my basement. I had no interest in going out, seeing my friends, making deliveries. I was compromised by everything I knew. I knew too much about my uncle. I knew things about him that a sixteen-year-old nephew should not have known. And when my mother invited him to our house for dinner—in an effort to bolster his spirits—I sat across the table from him and tried to suppress the feeling of an awkward bond. The bond two men have when they have been with the same woman. It wasn't the sort of bond I wanted to share with my forty-four-year-old uncle, especially under the circumstances. But the feeling was more powerful than my desire not to feel it. It was too easy to picture him with her. Everything my uncle did during dinner— talking, eating, drinking—reminded me that he had been with Natasha. The mouth he spoke with, the hands he ate with, his physical self, were the same mouth, hands, self that had been with Natasha.

Of those first few depressing days after Natasha left, the

dinner with my uncle was the worst. During that dinner he avoided the subject of Zina and Natasha entirely. It was the only thing on everyone's mind and so, characteristically, it was the only thing nobody mentioned. Instead my uncle gave a very long and detailed history of the Israeli-Palestinian conflict. Arafat, Rabin, Ben-Gurion, Balfour, Begin, Nasser, Sadat. I wondered what kept my uncle going. What life offered him. Why he didn't kill himself. Watching him, listening to him talk, I realized that there was nothing I could do for him. I felt better.

The following morning I ended my self-imposed seclusion and took the familiar walk to Rufus's. Weeks remained in my summer. There were books to read and whatever else the summer still had to offer. During my seclusion I had avoided all phone calls. Rufus had left typically cryptic messages, as did some of my other friends. Something in their voices intimated that there was excitement in our world. Activity was taking place without me. Conversations, discoveries, all sorts of important new things. Because of Natasha, I had removed myself from the common equation, and I was ready to return and accept my place within the social order.

Approaching Rufus's house, I wasn't surprised to see the pool company's van as well as a large truck brimming with dirt. Guys with wheelbarrows were carting dirt out from Rufus's yard and shoveling it into the truck. Teams of six landscapers shouldered ten-foot-long Doric columns in the opposite direction. The strains of Bizet's *Carmen* wafted from the backyard. The neighborhood had never seen anything like it.

In the backyard, I spotted most of my friends. Guys that had never held down a real job, guys like me who spent their days in basements reading, smoking, and engaging in self-abuse. They were fanned out across Rufus's yard, straining, digging, smoothing, lifting, side by side with the landscapers and pool installers. They looked very happy. Intimately involved. And already they had succeeded in transforming Rufus's yard. A massive hole, many feet deep, dominated the property. An orange plastic fence had been erected around the hole's circumference to keep the workmen and stoners from accidentally falling in.

Up on the deck, seated with one of the pool guys I had seen on my last visit, was Rufus. A blueprint was laid out on the table and both of them were hunched over it as though it were a battle plan. I mounted the steps to the deck and stood behind Rufus and waited for him to acknowledge me. Over his shoulder I could see the detail of the blueprint. There were columns, cypress trees, a fountain, and Rufus's hot tub. Rufus looked up as I bent closer to get a better look. For the briefest instant his face assumed an expression I had never seen before. At that moment I didn't understand what it meant, but I later recognized it as pity.

—Berman, what's the matter, you don't return calls anymore?

He rose and had me follow him down into the yard. I felt the onset of dread. Something about Rufus's posture alerted me to tragedy. It was then that I also realized that none of my friends had said anything to me. The yard was busy, but not so busy that none of them would have seen me. I had, after all, seen them. The sum of these impressions began to register. I knew that whatever it was, it was very bad and that I was trapped and helpless to avoid the damage. I sensed all of this as I descended from the deck and heard the screen door open. Using her hip, Natasha slid the door closed. She was carrying a tray with a pitcher of water and multicolored plastic glasses.

Rufus watched me for a reaction and then took me gently by the shoulder and out to the front of the house.

—Berman, this is why I asked you to call. I wanted to tell you on the phone, but it wasn't exactly the sort of thing I could leave on an answering machine.

Another team of landscapers passed us with a Doric column. I felt a compulsion to stick out my foot and trip them. To start a brawl, draw blood, break bones.

—She doesn't want to see you. I'm sorry about this, Berman. It's just the way it is.

I made way for the Doric column.

—How much do those things weigh?

—Not as much as you'd think. They're masonry and plaster, not marble. If they were marble I'd need slaves.

—I thought she was going to Florida.

—Come on, Berman, she's a fucking kid. How is she supposed to get to Florida? She barely speaks English. Either she's here or she's on the street.

—Right.

—She thinks you betrayed her. She's very principled. Anyway, she'll be safe here.

—That's one way to look at it.

—I hope you're not mad. It's not personal.

—I still have some of your books and maybe few grams of weed.

—That's cool. Don't sweat it. Consider them yours.

—What a great deal for me.

—That's a shitty attitude, Berman. You're smarter than that.

—I'm a fucking genius.

—Take care of yourself, Berman.

I lingered in front of Rufus's house after he left and

watched the wheelbarrows come and go. I waited for the workmen to bring in the last of the Doric columns and then walked home. In another country, under another code, it would have been my duty to return to Rufus's with a gun. But in the suburbs, at the end of my sixteenth summer, this was not an option. Instead, I resorted to a form of civilized murder. By the time I reached my house everyone in Rufus's yard was dead. Rufus, Natasha, my stoner friends. I would never see them again. By the time I got home I had already crafted a new identity. I would switch schools, change my wardrobe, move to another city. Later I would avenge myself with beautiful women, learn martial arts, and cultivate exotic experiences. I saw my future clearly. I had it all planned out. And yet, standing in our backyard, drawn by a strange impulse, I crouched and peered through the window into my basement. I had never seen it from this perspective. I saw what Natasha must have seen every time she came to the house. In the full light of summer, I looked into darkness. It was the end of my subterranean life.

CHOYNSKI

•

THE PALLIATIVE-CARE DOCTOR, a young Jewish guy in glasses, prodded around my grandmother's stomach and explained that the swelling wasn't only a result of fluid. Some of it was disease. Disease had now infiltrated her kidneys and pancreas. He said that it was a very horrible disease, this disease, but everybody in the room—except my grandmother—already knew approximately how horrible it was. My grandmother said *tank you* to the doctor and also said the word *hoff* several times. Her English was virtually nonexistent and I didn't think the doctor's Yiddish was good enough to understand that the word she kept repeating meant *hope*.

Outside, in the hall, the doctor explained that it was useless for me to wait around. It could be a month or it could be less, but there was no sense in my canceling my plane ticket. I thanked him and then returned to the living room to watch the second period of the hockey game. In the other room I could hear my mother and aunt lying to my grandmother about what the doctor had said.

The same summer that we were given the diagnosis I had gone to the induction ceremony at the International Boxing Hall of Fame in Canastota, New York. This is where I was told to check in with Charley Davis, who was recovering from a stroke but still lived independently in his house in San Francisco. Not that anybody knew very much, but if there was anyone who knew anything about Joe Choynski that person would be Charley Davis.

Joe Choynski was being inducted in the old-timers' category that day. Chrysanthemum Joe, Little Joe, the Professor, the California Terror: he was known as the greatest heavyweight never to win a title by the handful of people who still remembered that he'd ever been around. He was America's first great fighting Jew. He quoted Shakespeare in his correspondence. He was a friend to Negroes. Coolies on the San Francisco docks taught him to toughen his fists in pickle vats, which was why he never so much as chipped a bone—bare-knuckle or gloved. Legend had it that he also invented the left hook.

From Los Angeles, I called to find out that my grandmother hadn't had a proper stool in three days and that the enema produced only an insignificant pellet which took her an hour to pass. Afterward, in her exhaustion, she wasn't able to leave the bedroom until morning. Her dentist called to say that her dentures—which I had dutifully dropped off before leaving town—could not be repaired but needed to be replaced, and my aunt agreed to pay whatever it cost since neither she nor anyone else was prepared to tell my grandmother that she wouldn't be needing new dentures.

My aunt asked exactly where this God is, especially since my grandfather prays twice a day in synagogue. And my grandmother said that God will help, that the shark cartilage will help, that the naturopathic professor will help, that it just takes more time before the good cells start fighting the bad cells inside there.

Charley Davis lived in South San Francisco not far from
3Com Park. Back when 3Com Park was Candlestick Park,
Charley Davis covered the Giants and the fights for the *San
Francisco Chronicle*. His house was half a mile from the high-
way and set high on a street of identical houses. Charley let
me in and asked me to follow him into the living room.
He was wearing blue pajamas under a faded brown robe. He
dragged his left leg and his left arm hung as rigid as a pen-
guin's flipper. His house was covered in old fight posters and
pictures of guys I recognized and would have traded lives with
even though they were already dead. As Charley inched into
his armchair and organized his limbs, I concentrated on a
framed shot of the Johnson-Jeffries fight.

When he was settled, I sat down on the couch across from
him and told him that I was stuck with my Choynski re-
search. I pronounced the name the way he had taught me over
the phone: *Cohen-ski*. He asked me if I figured I could identify
Choynski in one of the pictures at the Johnson-Jeffries fight.
Choynski had worked Jeffries's corner for that Great White
Hope fight in Reno. After I passed that test we went through
our collective Choynski information.

—He was a candy puller.

—Yeah.

—Do you know what that is?

—Not really.

—Me neither.

—He was a blacksmith before he was a candy puller.

—He fought out of the California Club when he met
Corbett on the barge.

—When he worked in the candy factory he trained at the Golden Gate Club.

—His father was a publisher. Some Jewish paper.

—He had his own later, *Public Opinion*. Isadore N. Choynski. He had a bookstore. He graduated from Yale.

—His mother didn't like him boxing.

—He wore his hair long and got into plenty of fights on the docks.

—He lost those two fights to Goddard in Australia.

—He taught Jack Johnson what he needed to know to become champion when they had spent a month together in a Galveston jail in 1901.

The further we went on, the more we had to restrain ourselves from rushing into each other's arms for the joy of it. I mean, I almost rushed—Charley wasn't getting around that well anymore. Don't look for him in the Boston Marathon, he said.

There really wasn't that much material on Choynski, and I turned out to know more than Charley. Back then I was the world's greatest authority on Joseph B. Choynski, and I still didn't know him at all. I told Charley I didn't know where else to go, I'd run out of places to look for Choynski and didn't like to think that I'd never find him.

I didn't tell him about wanting to know another kind of everything about Choynski. I wanted to follow him as he walked home at night, I wanted to know what he smelled like, to hear the sound of his voice, to know the dimensions of his wife. I wanted to know if the reason he never had kids was because he had taken too low blows.

—Fighters then were like hobos. Fights were illegal almost everyplace. They just drifted around. There weren't any of those commissions back then and all those letters they have now—WBO, WBC, IBF, whatever the fuck they are. Look, some places boxers were celebrities, most places they were just trying to make a buck.

I was supposed to come back the next day so he could give me a picture of Choynski to copy. He could have had it ready that day but I also could have been full of shit and he didn't like to waste his time on morons.

After that day with Charley I did my tour of San Francisco. I looked up 1209 Golden Gate Avenue, where the Choynski house used to be. It had been destroyed in the 1906 earthquake. A new development was there in its place, based on old photographs and a general idea but built along a modern formula. The candy factory at Third and Stevenson was nowhere to be found and nobody knew where to look for the Golden Gate Club, although in the late 1880s it had stood on that very corner.

I went to the San Francisco Public Library and looked again through the old *San Francisco Call Bulletin* microfilm. I read about a six-day bicycle race at the Mechanics' Pavilion. The winner was a guy named Miller who rode an Eldridge-brand bicycle 18,000 times around the track for a total of 2,192 miles. This was February 1899, when Choynski fought Kid McCoy and lost the decision. After the fight Eddie Graney, "sportsman, politician, and Joe's best friend," suggested that Joe quit the fight game, since he was no longer the man he used to be.

Each day my grandmother lost something more of herself, as if the disease knew that one day had passed and the next had begun. One day she could sit in a chair in her bedroom, the next day she couldn't get out of bed, and the day after that she couldn't turn herself over. A nurse came every other day to look at her; another woman showed up every morning to clean the house and bathe her. Once, when everyone believed she could no longer get up, she walked halfway to the bathroom in the middle of the night, fell, and cut her cheekbone on the dresser.

I called and every word she said that day was reported to me, although, close to the end, she wasn't saying very much. One day my mother heard her moan and asked where it hurt and my grandmother replied her heart. My mother panicked because the doctors hadn't said anything about her heart. My grandmother said her heart hurt for what will happen to my grandfather after. As always, my mother assured her that she would get better. Idiot, my grandmother said, don't laugh at your mother, soon enough you'll be crying.

Charley had dedicated one bedroom entirely to his boxing memorabilia. He had an award from the Boxing Writers' Association of America and a picture of him receiving it in 1982. He had press passes from fights in Atlantic City, Tokyo, Sacramento, and other places. There were autographed pictures and framed shots of old-timers. In his closet, he had a filing system of cigar boxes, plastic lunch pails, and tackle boxes. There were gaps on the walls where he'd sold some of his pictures—protruding nails and whitish rectangles denoted absence. Five shots of Tunney and Dempsey had paid his medical bills.

After he fished around for the right cigar box Charley suffered another stroke and dropped everything on the floor. I wasn't fast enough to catch him on his way down, but his right shoulder hit the hardwood first and cushioned the blow to his head. He was still breathing but appeared unconscious. When he fell, Charley scattered some of his old press passes. One with a picture of him from the seventies landed on his right pajama leg. The picture testified to the fact that Charley had once been a handsome man.

Before her illness, I used to sit in my grandmother's apartment and listen to her gossip on the phone to her friends in Yiddish. I used to sit with her, my grandfather, and the rest of them as they talked about the war. Before the war they knew how to make ice skates out of wire, wood, and rope. My grandfather made them exactly the same way in Latvia as my great-uncle in Lithuania. Before the war, my grandmother recalled there was character called a *sharmanka* who went from town to town. He had an accordion and a little white mouse and he could predict the future. (In Russian he was called a *katarinshik*, my grandfather interrupted.) When the *sharmanka* came to her shtetl all the children ran after him and gave him a few pennies. But my grandmother believed that even if she had asked the right questions, she couldn't have changed the way things turned out.

Still, during the war they all saw miracles—which meant they remained alive while Germans died. God proved himself to them even though there was more of the same kind of evidence against Him.

Since they offered, I rode along in the ambulance with Charley. I sat in the back with two attendants. Charley was in bad shape for most of the ride, but by the time they stabilized him he had his own room, and I found myself lingering around the hospital waiting for I wasn't sure what. The doctor had started relying on me for information about Charley, and since I liked the idea of being a participant in the final drama of Charley's life, I gave the doctor the impression that I knew Charley better than I did.

When I checked in on him later that night Charley was awake but he couldn't speak. The doctor was asking him about his family. There were papers that the doctor needed signed, just in case. Charley could only communicate by writing things down on a pad with what was left of the motor functions in his right hand.

—Do you have anybody you want to contact?

Charley rolled his eyes to that. It was identical to a gesture that a perfectly healthy person would have made.

—Brothers, sisters? Children?

Charley moved his eyes away from the doctor to the other side of the room.

—If you have children, Mr. Davis, you should tell them. They would want to know about this. There may not be another chance.

Charley shook his head wearily. It didn't mean there weren't any children; it meant he wished the doctor would leave him alone. The doctor walked over to Charley's right side with the pad and a pencil. He held it in front of Charley's face and waited.

Charley wrote: JIM FRESNO.

—Is that his last name, Fresno, or is that where he is?

Charley shut his eyes and turned his back on the doctor.

. . .

There were eight James Davises listed in Fresno and only three of them were home. None of these had a father named Charley Davis in San Francisco. I left five messages for the other James Davises—four on machines and one with a Mexican cleaning lady.

After dinner I got a call from one of my James Davises who said he had a father in San Francisco named Charley Davis.

—What did your father do for a living?

—He was a sportswriter for the *Chronicle*. He wrote about men trying to knock each other's heads off.

—I think you should come to San Francisco.

Jim Davis wore khaki Dockers and a red golf shirt embroidered with the Promise Keepers logo. He had flakes of dry skin and an eyelash on the lenses of his glasses. He worked for a real estate brokerage, and he appeared at the hospital just after midnight.

Charley was sleeping when his son arrived and the doctor didn't think it was a good idea to wake him. By this point I was very familiar with the locations of the snack and coffee machines.

One of the first things Jim asked me was if I belonged to a church. I told him I did not. He asked if I had a personal relationship with Christ. His father, he said, never allowed Christ into his heart; he had never come to accept Christ's love.

We sat in the waiting area eating carrot muffins out of plastic packages and drinking coffee.

—I have a friend in my church group who was a trouble-maker as a kid and his dad worried about what would happen to him. His dad wasn't a religious man, he worked for the phone company in Sacramento. But his dad made a deal with him. He told my friend that if he went to church with him every Sunday for a year he'd get him anything he wanted. You know, within limits, but really anything. My friend, he agreed, except for Little League when that was on Sundays. And he did it. Both him and his dad, every Sunday for a year except Little League. And when the year was up his dad asked him what he wanted and you know what he said? He said I want you to promise to keep going to church with me. That the two of them would keep going to church together. Him and his dad.

As I listened to the story I tried to anticipate the ending. I had heard something similar from one of my Hebrew school teachers.

After Jim finished his story he wrote a list of verses that he was certain would help me to develop a personal relationship with Christ.

When Charley woke up, the doctor called Jim in and I decided it was time for me to go. A nurse caught up to me as I waited for the elevator and said I had to go see Charley right away. Charley was calling for me; he was getting excited, and I had to come right away.

Inside his father's room Jim was kneeling by the bed. He was weeping and repeating:

—Daddy, I love you; Jesus loves you. Jesus loves you very much, Daddy! Do you know Jesus loves you? Jesus loves you very much, Daddy!

The nurse held the pad so Charley could scrawl. Ignoring his son's hysterics, Charley wrote: MAKE SURE ABOUT MY THINGS.

I told him I would.

MAKE SURE JESUS DOESN'T GET THEM, he wrote.

In the elevator, my phone rang. It was well past one in the morning and I felt sick as soon as I heard it. I let it ring once more even though I could have picked it up. When I picked it up a man's voice without a Russian accent said hello. A doctor, I thought, although it didn't make sense.

—It's Jim Davis.

—Yeah, Jim, what is it?

—What do you mean, what is it? What happened to my father?

—What do you mean?

—What do you mean what do I mean? You called, didn't you?

—I don't understand. Where are you?

—In Fresno. Where the fuck do you think I am? Where the hell are you?

—I'm—

—What the fuck is going on?

—Are you sure you have the right number?

—Are you fucking sick? Whoever the fuck you are, you talked to my maid this afternoon.

Just after I hung up, the phone rang again. This time it was my cousin.

—Why was your phone busy?

—I don't know.

—Come home.

In the background I heard everyone crying. My mother was already reaching for the phone. She said in Russian:

—Kitten, babushka is gone. There is no more babushka.

· · ·

Charley's place was only fifteen minutes away from the airport. I went there first and found the Choynski picture he'd promised me. It was one I didn't already have. It had been taken in the early 1890s when Joe was at his peak. In the photo he is wearing black tights and his shoulders and arms are taut with muscle. I didn't feel bad taking it since I was sure Charley meant for me to have it anyway. For the rest of his things, I intended to call Canastota and the Hall of Fame.

There was a morning flight to Toronto and I slept for a few hours on Charley's couch before going to the airport. It occurred to me how, with technology, it was possible to never miss a funeral.

On the plane I read over Jim's list of verses for a personal relationship with Christ.

John 1:12	We can become Gods children
Rom 3:23	We are all sinners and need Gods grace
Hebrew 9:27	We ultimately must pay the consequences of our misdeeds
Revelation 3:20	We must open our heart to Jesus and ask Him to come into our life

At the bottom he left me his phone number and drew the sign of the cross.

I never called him or looked up the verses. At home we didn't own a New Testament, but I found the prayer I had loved best in Hebrew school. It was taught to me by a beautiful Sephardic woman who was also my fourth-grade Hebrew teacher. We sang it every morning during prayers.

From out of distress I called to God; with abounding relief, God answered me. The Lord is with me, I do not fear— what can man do to me? The Lord is with me among my helpers, I will see the downfall of my enemies. It is better to rely on the Lord than to trust in man. It is better to rely on the Lord than to trust in nobles. All the nations surrounded me, but in the Name of the Lord I will cut them down. They surrounded me, they encompassed me, but in the Name of the Lord I will cut them down. They surrounded me like bees, yet they shall be extinguished like fiery thorns; in the Name of the Lord I will cut them down. My foes repeatedly pushed me to fall, but the Lord helped me. God is my strength and song, and He has been a help to me. The sound of rejoicing and deliverance reverberates in the tents of the righteous, "The right hand of the Lord performs deeds of valor. The right hand of the Lord is exalted; the right hand of the Lord performs deeds of valor!"

It was a fighter's prayer.

They buried my grandmother in a plain pine box. By the end there was hardly anything left of her. In her final week she had been unable to eat, and ultimately it had become too painful for her to even swallow water. I was told that she had died unconscious, shrieking for breath with an IV in her arm.

During the funeral I only cried for my mother's sake, and before that a little because I saw my grandfather lost and weeping like an old Jew. Even when her pine coffin reverberated like a bass drum with the first shovelfuls of dirt, I was okay.

It was only later, that night, when I was on my hands and knees in the cemetery searching for her dentures in two feet of snow, that I wailed in Russian: *Babushka, babushka, g'dye tih, maya babushka?* Babushka, babushka, where are you, my babushka? I cried shamelessly, up to my elbows in the snow, looking for the new teeth which they had forgotten to bury with her. Bearing the dentures I had driven out into the worst blizzard since 1944 with neither a flashlight nor a shovel. I had gone to the cemetery even though my mother had forbidden it and even though Jewish law dictated that nobody was permitted at the grave for a month. But I felt that I was following other laws. And so I dug—first with purpose, then with panic. My hands burned and then went numb. Snow soaked through my shoes and pants. By the end, I didn't even want to bury the teeth anymore, I just wanted not to lose them.

MINYAN

·

AFTER MY GRANDMOTHER'S DEATH, my grandfather announced he wanted to move out of the apartment they had shared for ten years. Too many memories, and also, for one person, it was expensive. My mother and aunt filled out forms for subsidized housing and my grandfather was placed on a waiting list. If a spot opened up he would be able to save hundreds of dollars each month. Of course, the money wouldn't change his life. His needs were minimal. Tea, potatoes, cottage cheese, black bread, chicken, milk, preserves. My mother and aunt bought him his clothes at Moore's—a discount chain whose labels read: Made in Canada. He never traveled, never went to concerts or movies, and had no hobbies aside from the synagogue. That he had no immediate use for the money wasn't the point. When he was gone, the grandchildren would have more.

My grandmother's yartzheit came and went and my grandfather was still no closer to getting an apartment. Thousands were on the waiting list and there was no way of knowing how much longer he would have to wait. My mother told me a year wasn't that long, she had heard of others who had waited three or five. The waiting list outlived more applicants than she cared to mention. Sholom Zeydenbaum's son, Minka, received a letter a month after Sholom's death. Minka said he didn't know whether to laugh or cry. When he told the story, he laughed.

The system was inscrutable. At least in Russia you knew who to bribe.

But, unable to give up, my family sought angles. My mother made inquiries in the community. Apartments had been had. Others had experienced success. No doubt an apartment existed, and waited, like America, to be discovered. My father canvassed his patients in search of a lead. Many patients were the children of Polish Jews who had made their money in real estate. They owned buildings all over the city. Surely one of them could find a suitable place for an honest man, a war hero and a pious Jew. My uncle played his trump card and exploited a political connection from his days doing business with the new Russia. The man had been an ambassador, the man had served on the city council. Such a man must be able to help. My aunt wondered why it had to be so hard. Didn't all these people have parents of their own? Were their hearts made of stone? My uncle informed her that these people did indeed have parents of their own and that their parents were probably the reason why my grandfather couldn't get an apartment.

More months passed. A possibility here and a potential opportunity there. All of them came to nothing and my grandfather, never an optimist by nature, resigned himself to the fact that it was a lost cause. Some people had a talent for making things happen, he was not one of them. Once, during the war, he had had a chance to make some money. A man in Kyrgyzstan had a load of hats he wanted to move. Good woolen hats of a very desirable fashion. My grandfather and his brother had the inside track on the hats. One railway car to Moscow and they could have made a fortune. They could have been extremely wealthy men in Russia, but their father wouldn't let them do it. He was a very honest man. He never invited trouble. So the hats went to someone else—who naturally made a fortune—and my grandfather worked with his hands for the rest of his life. Like the hats, so the apartment. My grandfather entertained no illusions, unless, of course, they were illusions of exaggerated bleakness.

All along, at the margins of the apartment search, there was one possibility that neither fully materialized nor completely disappeared. A building owned by the B'nai Brith was in fact subsidized. It was only a short bus ride from my grandfather's current building. It faced a park. Most of the people in the building were either widows or widowers. On the ground floor was a common room where concerts were occasionally held. My grandfather had a few acquaintances who lived there and he felt the building would present him with more social opportunities. Since my grandmother's death he had seen less and less of their old friends. My grandmother had always been the one to make the phone calls and the arrangements, and now that she was gone, he felt that most of their friends had indeed been her friends. On his own, my grandfather found it hard to break the old patterns.

The B'nai Brith building seemed the perfect solution. And, it appeared that there was a slim chance that he could gain a preferential place on their waiting list. Word had spread at the tiny Russian community synagogue that my grandfather was looking to find an apartment. This word had reached a popular and well-respected rabbi who knew my grandfather to be a pious man and regular synagogue attendee. This very fact made him an attractive candidate since the B'nai Brith building had its own one-room synagogue which was no longer drawing a minyan for Friday night and Saturday morning services. I couldn't believe that, in a building whose entire population consisted of old Jews, they couldn't find ten men, but my grandfather insisted that it was true. Even though the building was Jewish, the people were old. Some were sick, some were atheists, and more than half of the residents were women. It was a serious problem. The synagogue was Orthodox, and without ten Jewish men, they could not hold proper services.

Since I was conveniently between jobs, it was my responsibility to drive my grandfather to the B'nai Brith building to meet with Zalman, the synagogue's gabbai. Zalman was a Romanian Jew who spoke Russian, Hebrew, Yiddish, and quite a lot of English. For years he had overseen the day-to-day running of the synagogue. If my grandfather could impress upon him his level of religious commitment, then Zalman would be able to use his influence with the building's manager. The manager was sympathetic to the synagogue's plight and might be willing to manipulate the waiting list in order to bring in the right kind of resident. In other words, a spiritual ringer.

On the way to meet with Zalman my grandfather repeated that it probably wouldn't do any good. If Zalman could do anything, he would have done it long ago. The trip was a waste of time. Nevertheless, he clutched the letter of recommendation that the rabbi had written for him. I told him not to worry. He replied that when you got to be his age there was no longer much to worry about. Everything was in God's hands. Who are we to know His plans? What is getting or not getting an apartment compared to losing a wife? God does what He does for His own reasons. If it was meant for us to get the apartment, then it would happen, if not, then not. What could anyone do? I said he could pray, but he didn't get the joke.

The synagogue was indeed one room which was divided into two sections by a flimsy latticework partition. On the left was the women's section; on the right the men's. Each side could hold thirty people. Zalman pointed out what went where. Here the prayer books, there the tallisim are folded, over there the ark and the Torah. He opened up the doors so that we could take a look at the scrolls in their velvet cover. My grandfather said it was a very good synagogue and gave Zalman the rabbi's letter. Zalman promised to do what he could, so long as we understood that there was no telling when an apartment might open up. Did we understand what it meant for an apartment to become available in such a place? Unfortunately, my grandfather said, he understood very well.

On the way out, Zalman escorted us through the lobby. We passed two Russian seniors who studied us with unconcealed malice. Zalman explained that these were two of the ones who wouldn't come. Atheists, Zalman said. One a product of Stalin, the other of Hitler. But what do you say to a man who asks you where was God when the Germans were shooting his parents and throwing them in a hole? It isn't a pleasant conversation. And who here didn't lose someone to the Nazis? I lost my grandparents, three beautiful sisters, uncles, aunts, cousins. So what am I supposed to do, let the bastards win? Because who wins if a Jew doesn't go to synagogue? I'll tell you who: Hitler.

Three Russians who didn't understand Hebrew sat in the back of the synagogue. One was missing an arm. Two Polish Jews sat in front of them. One had his place by the partition so that he could stretch his bad leg, the other kept his walker near for emergency trips to the washroom. I was between them and the front row where my grandfather sat with two other men. Herschel, a Holocaust survivor from Lithuania, sat beside my grandfather, and Itzik, a taxi driver from Odessa, sat beside Herschel. Zalman was at a small table beside the ark. On the other side of the partition were half a dozen women. There was no rabbi and so the responsibilities for the service were divided between Zalman, my grandfather, and Herschel. The task of lifting the heavy scrolls fell to me, as I was the only one with the strength to do it. The Saturday morning services started at nine and lasted for three hours. Most of the old Jews came because they were drawn by the nostalgia for ancient cadences, I came because I was drawn by the nostalgia for old Jews. In each case, the motivation was not tradition but history.

After services everyone went to the common room for a kiddush. Zalman brought a bottle of kosher sweet wine and a honey cake. The Russian man with one arm contributed a mickey of cheap vodka. It takes only one arm to pour and only one arm to drink. Thank God, he said, at least here it is no disadvantage to be a one-armed man.

One of the women distributed the wine in small paper cups and also circulated a dish with the slices of cake. When everyone had drunk their wine and munched their cake, they wished one another a *gut Shabbos* and wandered alone or in small groups back to their particular lives.

On those mornings I accompanied my grandfather back to his new apartment, where we drank tea and played checkers. The new apartment was slightly smaller than the old. The brown sofa had been sold and replaced with a blue one. The brown sofa hadn't folded out; the blue one did. (Now, in the event of familiar tragedy, my mother and aunt wouldn't have to spend the accursed nights on the living room floor.) The bedroom remained identical and in the kitchen were the same chipped plates and the same enamel Soviet bowls good for warming soup. I would spend a few hours with my grandfather, his only visitor all week. The change of locale hadn't done much to improve his social situation. For every reason to leave his apartment he could always find ten to stay where he was. My grandfather had expected Zalman to make more of an effort, but Zalman was always preoccupied with unspecified concerns. He also had a wife. Only Herschel, the survivor who sat beside my grandfather, had extended invitations—to come over for tea, to read some Yiddish poetry, to play cards, to go for a walk in the park. He is a very intellectual man, my grandfather said. A professor.

Despite this, my grandfather had yet to accept any of Herschel's invitations. He would go, he said, it was only that every time he was invited something needed to be done. Once he had been salting pickles, another time he had needed to mend a pair of shoes, yet another time he had had an appointment to get his toenails cut. But when the time was good he planned to go. Other people said things about Herschel and Itzik, but he had lived a long life without listening to those kinds of people. Who can know about the truth between two people? Both had had wives. Itzik had two children. What's to say that they aren't even cousins? Who knows? Would someone think to say a word if two cousins shared an apartment?

The following Saturday I noticed how, when Itzik coughed, Herschel placed a hand on his shoulder. I also noticed an undercurrent of disapproval emanating from the back of the room. After Herschel read from the Torah the other men took his outstretched hand without enthusiasm. Previously undetected signals were everywhere. It seemed less like a coincidence when Itzik and Herschel were the last to receive their paper cups of wine. It was evident that the one-armed man barely acknowledged Herschel as he happily made an observation in Yiddish. Itzik sat alone at a table, his thick chest spasmodically wracked by terrible hacking. Young person, he said, could you bring me some water? The devil has me by the throat.

When I returned from the water fountain with a paper cup, Herschel was standing beside Itzik. At the front of the room Zalman was announcing a Chanukah party. I handed the cup to Itzik. Herschel asked me how tall I was. In his shtetl I would have been a giant. You can only get so big on cabbage, he said. His brother, a Communist before it was a good idea to be one, had been big for a Jew. He'd broken the arm of a Pole who had cracked Herschel's skull. The Pole was a blacksmith's apprentice. He had arms like legs. Herschel wondered if I would be able to come to their apartment and change a lightbulb. Itzik used to do it but it wasn't such a good idea for him now that he wasn't feeling well. And even standing on their tallest chair, Herschel wasn't big enough to reach. You could only sit in the dark for so long. Herschel spoke to me in English. Itzik, when he spoke, spoke to me in Russian. They spoke Yiddish to each other.

While beating me twice at checkers, my grandfather told me what he knew about Herschel and Itzik. They had been neighbors in another building. Their wives had been friends. Herschel had come to Canada in 1950. During the war Herschel's wife hid in a cellar; Herschel was sent to Auschwitz.

Like our family, Itzik left the Soviet Union in 1979. He had been a successful man in Odessa. He drove a cab. He had his own car. Sometimes he went for long trips with a full trunk and when he came back the trunk was empty. People said he brought dollars with him from Odessa. How else could he have bought his own taxi so soon after coming to Canada? Later he had three cars and rented them out. He wasn't like

my grandfather and the other old men. On the first of the
month he didn't have his nose in a mailbox sniffing for gov-
ernment envelopes.

Four years ago Itzik's wife died. He put himself on a waiting list for a subsidized apartment. The next year Herschel's
wife also died. Herschel also put himself on a waiting list. But
unlike Itzik, Herschel couldn't sit and wait. Even though he
was no newcomer to the country, he had no money. He was
an intellectual, a man of ideas. Not a practical man. Without
his wife's check he could barely afford to pay for the apartment. So Herschel moved into Itzik's apartment. Maybe Itzik
did it as a mitzvah, because everyone knew he didn't need the
money. But then again, a man loses a wife, another man loses
a wife—this is an unimaginable loneliness. Who knows who
is helping who? One hand washes the other.

So when Itzik finally got this subsidized apartment Herschel came too. Again, what choice did he have? To pay for
Itzik's apartment was no different than paying for his old
apartment. In other words, impossible. And by then they had
been living together for two years. They move in here and people talk. Two men in a one-bedroom apartment. Old people
are no better than children. Worse, because they should know
better. But what can you expect from old Jews? We come from
little villages; we come from poor families. What kind of edu-
cation did we get? How many of us finished school? By fourteen you start working. You get maybe eight years of school.
The rest you learn from life.

I knocked and Herschel opened the door. He was wearing a
white cotton undershirt and a pair of faded trousers. His body
showed the effects of prostate treatment. The hormones had

atrophied his muscles and made his breasts grow. They hung loosely beneath his undershirt. He invited me in. He had a pair of slippers ready for me. The slippers were probably a little small, Herschel said, they weren't accustomed to giant visitors. Itzik sat on the couch in front of the television. He was seized by another fit of coughing and then strained to catch his breath. Look, the workman is here, he said. He is joking with you, Herschel said, this is how he jokes. When you're done with the light, Itzik said, you could take a look at the toilet.

I helped Herschel carry a chair from the kitchen. He held it as I removed the fixture and unscrewed the dead bulb. Can you believe we had no light here for three weeks, Herschel said. If you can do something, it only takes a minute, but if you can't do it, it stays like that forever. He threw the switch and marveled at the light. Wonderful, he said.

I trailed after Herschel as he went into the bedroom. There were two night tables flanking the queen-size bed. Each one supported a night-lamp. A small stack of books was piled on one of them. A glass of water rested on the other. Herschel went over to the one with the books and retrieved his wallet. He returned to me holding a five-dollar bill which I refused to take. It was late in the afternoon and I could also not accept his offer of tea. He thanked me repeatedly as he escorted me out into the hallway. As Herschel closed the door Itzik clutched his knees and steadied himself against another barrage of coughs.

The next Saturday was Chanukah and Itzik did not come down for the service. Without Itzik there were only nine men and so Zalman stood in front of the building and attempted to convince Semitic-looking passersby to come inside. He spent a half hour in the cold before two blackhats, a father and son, agreed to come in and help. When Zalman returned the three Russians in the back were already putting on their coats. Zalman glared at them and they sat back down. Because of the delay everyone was anxious. The service lurched, Zalman stumbled through the Torah reading, the women kibbitzed behind their partition, the Russians in the back complained about the time. When it was Herschel's turn to approach the Torah he asked Zalman to say a prayer for Itzik. He pledged eighteen dollars to the synagogue and stood solemnly, his hands shaking, as Zalman asked God to deliver Itzik from his illness and provide him with a full recovery.

The events of the morning put a damper on the Chanukah party. Nevertheless, Zalman's wife brought jelly donuts and the women passed them around on greasy napkins. I sat with my grandfather and Herschel as Zalman sang Chanukah songs. A few of the women joined in, although some could only hum the melody. Most of the others sat in their coats, their lips gleaming with oil and speckled with sugar, waiting for the opportunity to leave. Herschel asked if he could have a second donut to take upstairs to Itzik. Not that Itzik could eat it. It was hard to imagine, Herschel said, such a man. A real Odessa character, right out of the pages of Babel. He had even grown up on Babel's street. As a young boy Itzik had carted watermelons for Babel's uncle. What hadn't he done in his life? At thirteen he was working two shifts in a munitions factory. At seventeen he was at the front. He fought the Germans, he survived the Communists, he had an appetite for the world—and now, he didn't even have the strength to eat a donut.

As Itzik lay dying, strange and not-so-strange visitors appeared at Zalman's door. Zalman's apartment was on the same floor as Itzik's and these visitors no doubt heard the sound of coughing and rasping as it echoed through the hallway. In the last days, Itzik's son came from New Jersey to sit at his father's bedside. Many years had passed since he had seen or spoken with his father. Herschel stayed mostly in the kitchen cooking their meals and reading at the table. To allow Itzik and his son some privacy, Herschel spent several hours each day at my grandfather's. As he waited for the elevator to ride the four floors up to my grandfather's apartment, Herschel saw the people who knocked on Zalman's door. Those who knew him avoided his eyes.

Seated at my grandfather's table, Herschel seemed oblivious to the conspiracies that were threatening to turn his tragedy into disaster. He spoke about how wonderful it was that Itzik's son had finally returned to his father. No matter what happens, in the end a father is a father and a son is a son. His own regret was never having children. But after the Holocaust there were two types of people. There were those who felt a responsibility to ensure the future of the Jewish people, and then there were those, like Herschel's wife, who had been convinced that the world was irrefutably evil. Those were the two kinds, Herschel said, and as always he was neither one nor the other. For him, the world held neither mission nor meaning, only the possibility of joy. But because of the way he was, for the same reasons that he never had any money or became an important man, he allowed his wife to decide for them. He had rationalized that if joy existed in the world, then joy would continue to exist even if he didn't have a child. He was capable of these rationalizations, he said. His wife wasn't. She had made a decision in a Polish cellar and no amount of America could change her mind. He could understand her, Herschel said. He could also understand Itzik's son, and the people in the building who wouldn't meet his eyes. He could understand all of them. That was his problem, he said, he could understand everybody.

Itzik died on a Friday night and the funeral was held on Sunday. To ensure a minyan at the grave site, Zalman insisted that all of the synagogue regulars attend. I drove my grandfather, Herschel, and two of the old women to the chapel. Zalman came with his wife and the two Polish Jews. Itzik's son called Itzik's three cabbies and they brought everyone else. Aside from the people from the synagogue and the cabbies, almost nobody else came. Itzik had lived in Toronto for twenty years but hadn't had much to do with anyone after his wife died. The rabbi who had written my grandfather the letter of recommendation delivered the eulogy. He had not known Itzik well and made no secret of it. Zalman wrote some notes on a loose piece of paper and the rabbi studied the sheet before speaking. Itzik had been an unusual man, the rabbi said. He came to this country already an old man and had become successful. He had his own business and never asked anyone for anything. He supported his family and always gave money to the Jewish Russian community. In his last years he rediscovered his Jewish roots. For two years he never missed a Saturday service. Not looking at the sheet, the rabbi added that with the passing of Itzik the world lost another piece of the old Jewish life. His death was a tragedy not only for the people who loved Itzik but for all Jews everywhere.

After the rabbi spoke he asked if there was anyone who wanted to say anything more about Itzik. Herschel, who sat between me and my grandfather, wiped his eyes and looked over at Itzik's son. Itzik's son did not look up from the floor. Nobody moved and the rabbi shifted nervously beside Itzik's coffin. He looked around the room and asked again if there wasn't someone who had a few words to say about Itzik's life. If someone had something to say and sat in silence, they would regret it. Such a time is not the time for shyness. Itzik's spirit was in the room. To speak a kind word about the man would be a mitzvah. Finally, using my knee for support, Herschel raised himself from the pew and slowly made his way to the front of the chapel. Each of Herschel's steps punctuated silence. His worn tweed jacket and crooked back delivered a eulogy before he reached the coffin. His posture was unspeakable grief. What could he say that could compare with the eulogy of his wretched back?

Facing the room, Herschel composed himself and spoke clearly. Itzik was my last and dearest friend. Hitler killed my family and I never had children. When my wife died I thought I would be alone until God decided it was finally time to take me also. That Itzik was my dear friend these last years was the blessing of my old age. Without him I don't know what would have become of me. He was a wonderful man. He was an honest man. He was a strong man. He said not one word he didn't mean. I will miss him like I would miss my right arm. Living a long life is both a blessing and a curse. Today it is a curse. I don't know if it will ever again feel like a blessing.

At the cemetery, there were two-foot-high snowbanks. The earth from Itzik's grave was frozen in clumps and piled slightly higher than the snowbanks. The gravediggers had cleared a semicircle around the grave. Herschel stood by himself. Itzik's son held a shovel, another shovel was lodged in the frozen mound. The old people stamped their feet and wiped their noses. Zalman sang the prayer for the dead and the rabbi said some other prayers. Everyone dropped a hard earthen clod onto the lowered coffin. Then the rabbi, Itzik's son, and I filled the grave. Digging into the mound was like striking concrete. Each thrust sent a shock through my shoulders. Iztik's son stopped to rest but never relinquished his shovel. The rabbi and I would each dig for a minute and rest for a minute. It took nearly twenty minutes to finish the job. By the end sweat had stiffened my hair and milky icicles hung from the rabbi's beard.

As everyone stomped back through the snow toward the cars, Itzik's son thanked me for helping to bury his father. He hadn't said a word to me before. The only time I heard him speak was when he had asked the rabbi how he was to pay him for the service. Ahead of us the old people tottered through the snow. They walked in twos and threes, their arms linked to steady one another. Itzik's son stopped and watched them. Look at them, he said, who knows how many they robbed and cheated and screwed? He turned back toward Itzik's grave. He spent seven years in jail, my father, did you know that? I have brothers and sisters all over Russia. I don't even know how many. For him nothing was forbidden. That was my father, you understand? He raised his fist to his face. He was like this, Itzik's son said. He drove his fist into a snowbank. He looked at me to see if I understood. I nodded that I understood. Like this, he repeated, his fist in the snowbank.

No death in the building went unnoticed and Itzik's was anticipated. The people who had knocked on Zalman's apartment now slipped envelopes under the door. A bottle of vodka was left on his threshold. There were many in the building who disapproved of this behavior. My grandfather overheard conversations. But even those who disapproved felt they had no choice but to act. Everyone knew someone on the waiting list. Not to act was to guarantee that only people without principles would succeed in getting Itzik's apartment. The people with principles came to see Herschel as he sat shivah for Itzik. They brought eggs and bagels and honey cake and apologized for what they had to do. Herschel said he understood. He understood it had nothing to do with him.

For the week Herschel sat shivah Zalman refused to make any decisions. Still, everywhere he went that week, Zalman was oppressed with desperate stories. He had to understand. The list was, figuratively speaking, a cage, old Jews peered out through its bars and stretched their plaintive hands out to Zalman for salvation. It was no longer a secret that Zalman had the manager's ear and that soon enough the manager would come to him looking for a suggestion. Everyone also knew that Zalman needed to fill another place at the synagogue. With Iztik's death and not counting me, he was down to eight regulars. All kinds of pressure were being applied. The one-armed Russian man swore he would stop attending services if his brother-in-law was not allowed to take Itzik's apartment. His brother-in-law was a good Jew. He lived in an overpriced apartment. His building was full of blacks. He had diabetes. Why should he have to suffer because of Herschel? Just because this one shared a bed with another man he should be rewarded with an apartment? In Russia he would have been given ten years! And if this was the kind of synagogue Zalman was running, he'd sooner go to church than sit through another service.

Others appealed to Zalman with dubious temptations. Word had spread. Men who had never set foot inside the synagogue pledged regular attendance if only Zalman helped their deserving relatives. Zalman should do the math. In one move he would fill two spots. Sure, they hadn't come before, but now they would repay Zalman's mitzvah with one of their own. It was only fair. They had nothing against Herschel, but what right did he have to the apartment? Was he Itzik's wife? Is this the kind of world we were living in?

On Saturday morning more than twenty men appeared for the service. Almost as many women settled in behind the partition. Despite the air of sinister motivations, the room was transformed and Zalman walked through the aisles with a sense of purpose. He threw himself into the service with exceptional vigor. He sang out page numbers in Russian and Yiddish. He called the new attendees up to the Torah. Everyone made an effort at making an effort. Zalman. The new attendees. Voices battled each other for distinction. Herschel sat as usual beside my grandfather. He sang loud, his voice mingling with those of the others. The synagogue swelled with beautiful and conflicting prayer. God in His heaven was left to sort it out.

After the service Herschel followed me to my grandfather's apartment. My grandfather brought out the checkerboard and Herschel watched as we played. He preferred chess, he said, but he had always liked that all the pieces in checkers looked the same. It appealed to his socialist sensibilities. As if there was nothing else to talk about, Herschel looked over my shoulder as I contemplated moves. He dunked crackers into his tea and hummed a vague Yiddish-sounding melody. We played one game and then another. Herschel watched as if engrossed. He applauded clever moves and clucked his tongue at my mistakes. I finally asked him what he intended to do. He said he didn't know. What could he do? He'd lived a long life. So many things had happened. God had always watched over him. Why would He desert him now? He was on the waiting list like everyone else. Maybe his name would come up? What was the point of talking about it? You lived as you lived while you lived. Today he was drinking tea and watching checkers, why ruin a nice afternoon worrying about tomorrow?

I left Herschel with my grandfather. They were setting up the board for a game. Herschel was remembering how, so many years ago, his brother carved beautiful birch checker pieces. The Sabbath elevator arrived and I climbed aboard. The elevator descended, stopping automatically on every floor. Two floors down Zalman joined me in the elevator. He thanked me again for coming to the services. If he had more people like me, he wouldn't have any problems. I told him I was sorry about his problems. The laws were clear, he said. The old rabbis weren't fools. What do you need for a minyan? Ten Jewish men. The elevator stopped on his floor. Zalman stepped out. He had more to say. I followed him to his apartment and told him I wanted to know what he would do with Herschel.

Zalman looked up and down the hall to make sure we were alone. His eyes shone with intensity. Let me tell you, I am not a stupid man. I have my own opinions, but I am in charge of the synagogue. Do you think I liked the business with Itzik and Herschel? You shouldn't speak ill of the dead, but Itzik was a difficult man. And there are people who say they know very well why Herschel has no children. But for two years they came. I never said a word. Because my job is to have ten Jewish men. Good, bad, it doesn't matter. Ten Jewish men. Only God can judge good from bad. Here the only question is Jew or not. And now I am asked by people here who never stepped into a synagogue to do them a favor. They all have friends, relatives who need an apartment. Each and every one a good Jew. Promises left and right about how they will come to synagogue. I've heard these promises before. And they say, With so many good Jews who need apartments, why should Herschel be allowed to stay? This is not my concern. My concern is ten Jewish men. If you want ten Jewish saints, good luck. You want to know what will happen to Herschel? This. They should know I don't put a Jew who comes to synagogue in the street. Homosexuals, murderers, liars, and thieves—I take them all. Without them we would never have a minyan.

ACKNOWLEDGMENTS

Leonard Michaels (1933–2003), Wyatt Mason, Hannah Young